STARSCAPE BOOKS BY DAVID LUBAR

Flip

Hidden Talents

*In the Land of the Lawn Weenies
and Other Warped and Creepy Tales*

INVASION OF THE ROAD WEENIES

AND OTHER WARPED AND CREEPY TALES

INVASION OF THE ROAD WEENIES

AND OTHER WARPED AND CREEPY TALES

DAVID LUBAR

A TOM DOHERTY ASSOCIATES BOOK

NEW YORK

J
FIC
LUB

INVASION OF THE ROAD WEENIES
AND OTHER WARPED AND CREEPY TALES

Copyright © 2005 by David Lubar

A Starscape Book
Published by Tom Doherty Associates, LLC
175 Fifth Avenue
New York, NY 10010

www.starscapebooks.com

Library of Congress Cataloging-in-Publication Data

Lubar, David
Invasion of the road weenies : and other warped and creepy tales / David Lubar.—1st ed.
     p. cm.
Summary: A collection of thirty-five stories featuring such horrors as a monstrous Halloween
costume, a midnight visit to a graveyard, and a hearing-impaired genie. Includes author's notes on
how he got his ideas for these stories.
"A Tom Doherty Associates Book."
ISBN 0-765-31447-9 (acid-free paper)
EAN 978-0-765-31447-5
1. Horror tales, American. 2. Children's stories, American. [1. Horror stories. 2. Short
stories.] I. Title.

PZ7.L96775Inv 2005
[Fic]—dc22
            2005045116

First Edition: September 2005

Printed in the United States of America

0 9 8 7 6 5 4 3 2 1

For Kathleen Doherty,
who embodies all that is good and right
and magical in publishing

CONTENTS

CONTENTS

ACKNOWLEDGMENTS

Big thanks to Jonathan Schmidt, who put the first batch of Weenies into the oven and into the Starscape line. Huge thanks to Susan Chang for caring about every single word. Awestruck thanks to Bill Mayer for his amazing covers. Never-ending thanks to all the teachers who use my stories in their classrooms and all the librarians who place my books into the hands of readers. And, finally, thanks on a bun with lots of relish to everyone who helps make sure that the art of the short story is alive and well. That list is endless, but begins with those writers who still care about plots, stretches across a universe of publishers, anthologists, and editors, and ends right where it should with enthusiastic readers, such as you.

INVASION OF THE ROAD WEENIES

AND OTHER WARPED AND CREEPY TALES

THE LAST HALLOWEEN

Aren't you going out for trick or treat?" Jennifer's mom asked two weeks before Halloween. "If you want me to make a costume, we'd better start soon."

"I'm getting kind of old for that," Jennifer said. "Maybe I'll skip it this year."

"Are you sure? I thought you loved to go out."

Jennifer nodded. "I'm pretty sure." She'd been thinking about it ever since last year—ever since those older kids had stolen her candy and chased her down the street. As much as she loved Halloween, it just wasn't worth the risk. Monster terror was fun. Real terror wasn't.

"There's still time for me to make a costume," her mom said a week before Halloween.

"Thanks. But I think I'll stay home and hand out candy." *That might even be fun*, Jennifer thought. She liked seeing the little kids in their cute costumes. Her enthusiasm faded as she realized the older kids would come to her door, too—the ones who didn't even bother with real costumes. The ones who were just out to get as much candy as they could.

"Last chance," Jennifer's mom said the day before Halloween. "I can still put something together."

Jennifer looked out the window at the leaf-strewn streets that would soon be filled with costumed kids. "No thanks," she said.

But on Halloween, as the day fell dark and the smallest trick-or-treaters emerged from their houses like ants spilling from a hill, Jennifer wondered if it was too late to change her mind.

She had good memories of her first Halloween. It wasn't fair to have nothing but bad memories about her last one. But that awful Halloween didn't have to be her last one. Not if she went out now.

Costume, Jennifer thought, rummaging through her closet. Nothing. Sure, she could throw together a hippie outfit, or do some sort of clown makeup, but that wasn't good enough. That wasn't special.

She tried the basement. The sound of the doorbell drifted down from upstairs. As Jennifer scanned the piles of boxes stacked along a wall, the flash of a gold latch caught her eye.

Her great grandmother's old trunk sat shoved in a corner beneath moldy boxes of baby toys and a stack of canning jars. Jennifer vaguely remembered looking in the trunk when they'd first moved to the house.

She uncovered the trunk and unlatched the lid. A dusty smell of ancient cloth tickled her nose as she sorted through the contents. Just old dresses. Nice enough, but not the sort of costume she wanted. There was a hat with a veil—thin black gauze that covered the face of the wearer. *This might work in an emergency,* she thought. Still, she'd hoped to find something better.

Jennifer found nothing else. But, as she started to close the lid, she realized something was wrong. The outside of the trunk seemed deeper than the inside. She emptied the trunk and knocked her fist against the bottom. Instead of a solid whack, she was rewarded with a hollow thump. Excited, she pushed and pressed until she discovered the right spot. The false bottom popped up.

Jennifer held her breath as she lifted the wood panel, wondering what treasures she might find.

Gloves. That was all. One pair of black leather gloves. Jennifer noticed a folded slip of paper tucked between the fingers. She opened the slip and read the handwritten words out loud, "Special gloves for a special night."

The doorbell rang again. Jennifer heard a chorus of young voices shouting "Trick or treat!" Halloween was slipping past her like hourglass sand.

Jennifer grabbed the hat. Not a great costume, but it would have to do. On a whim, she grabbed the gloves, too. After all, it was a special night, even if she didn't have a special costume. She slipped the gloves over her hands. They fit like she'd worn them for years. She put on the hat. The veil cut her off from the world, filtering everything through a dark curtain.

Jennifer ran upstairs and grabbed her Halloween bag.

"I'm going out," she called to her mom.

"Have fun, dear. Be careful."

She dashed into the crisp air of the last night in October. As she knocked on her first door and got her first piece of candy, Jennifer knew she'd made the right decision. She traveled the familiar streets, following a pattern she'd worked out over the years.

At most houses, she heard the same question. "What an interesting costume. What are you?"

"Just a veiled lady," Jennifer told them.

She reached Pritchard Street. A dead end. The best path was down one side and up the other. She went to the first house on the right, and then the second.

As she left the second house, she heard the footsteps behind her. Footsteps and whispers. She took a quick glance over her shoulder at the hovering shapes. Taller kids, bigger kids. Though she hated to break the pattern, Jennifer crossed the street.

They followed. Going to each house right after her. Playing with her the way a cat plays with a mouse. They had time. She was trapped.

Jennifer crossed the street again.

They crossed, too.

And again.

Jennifer gripped her bag with her right hand, feeling the plastic handle bite against her palm through the thin leather of the gloves. *I'm just going to walk back to the corner,* she told herself. She'd go past them, and everything would be fine.

Forcing herself to look straight ahead, she took a step toward them. Crude laughs bubbled from the cluster of kids.

"Trick or treat," the boy in front said in a nasty, mocking voice. His only costume was a football shirt. Behind him, another boy, the tallest of the group, wore a motorcycle jacket.

"Gonna share?" the boy in front asked.

Jennifer avoided his eyes.

He stepped closer and reached toward her bag.

Jennifer put her left hand out, as if this motion had the power to stop them. She froze as the oddest sound punctured the night.

Thwick . . . thwick . . . thwick . . . thwick . . . thwick.

Claws, black as coal and sharp as needles, sprouted from her fingertips.

"Just give me the bag," the boy said.

Jennifer gave him the claws instead.

He screamed and clutched at his ripped shirt. The others took a step toward her. Jennifer flicked her arm out and slashed ribbons from the tall boy's leather jacket. She slashed flesh, too, but only enough to warn him off, only enough to make him think twice the next time he considered stalking a victim.

Even in the dark, the others saw enough to know what she had done.

They turned and fled. But not before Jennifer had flicked her wrist a final time, gutting their bags and spilling candy on the street.

The claws retracted.

Jennifer left the spilled candy for the little ones to find. She'd already received her reward. She finished her path along the street.

At the final house, a woman said, "My, my, that's a lovely costume. What are you?"

"Justice," Jennifer whispered.

"What?" the woman asked.

"Just a veiled lady," Jennifer said.

Her bag was nearly full. Normally, that was when she'd return home. But there were other kids out there like her, alone and vulnerable. And there were other gangs like the one she'd met.

Jennifer stayed on the streets until the last porch light went dark. Finally, she headed home.

"Did you have a good time?" her mother asked.

Jennifer nodded, sending a ripple through the veil. She removed the hat and gloves. "I think this was the best Halloween ever. I can't wait until next year."

"Well, just let me know ahead of time if you want a costume," her mother told her.

"I'll stick with this one," Jennifer said. "It's kind of fun. And it fits me really well."

BED TINGS

I was having a rotten day. First thing in the morning, I broke my camera. I know I shouldn't have left it on the floor right next to my bed, but that doesn't do me much good now. Then, right after breakfast, I accidentally dropped my toothbrush in the toilet.

When I told my friend Pauli what had happened, he said, "Well, it's almost over."

"What do you mean?"

"My grandma says that bad things happen in threes," Pauli told me. "You've had two bad things happen, so you've just got one more to get through and it's over."

"That's silly," I said.

I liked Pauli's grandma. She baked great cookies, and she always used lots of chocolate chips. But she was full of superstitions. And her accent was so thick, I had a hard time understanding her when she talked. She said *mek* instead of *make*, and *true* instead of *through*. I could just hear her telling Pauli that bad things happen in threes, but it would sound like *Bed tings heppen en treeze*. No matter how she said it, it was just a superstition.

"It might be silly," Pauli told me, "but if I were you, I'd be careful today."

"Yeah, right." I wasn't too worried. "Come on, let's play ball." I got my basketball from the garage and started to dribble it down the driveway.

The ball broke on the second bounce.

It just burst and went flat. I'd never seen a basketball do that.

"Bad thing," Pauli said.

"Shut up," I told him. But then I realized something. If bad things happen in threes, the bad part of my day was over. "I'm safe now," I said. "Watch this."

I got the ladder and climbed up the side of my house. Then I closed my eyes and ran along the top of the roof.

"Careful," Pauli shouted.

"Don't worry." I really felt great. It was wonderful knowing that nothing bad could happen to me now. I stood on one leg and spun around.

"Come on, get down," Pauli said.

"Okay." I went to the lowest part of the roof and jumped to the lawn. Naturally, I landed without any trouble.

For the rest of the day, I pushed my luck, and it held. As evening fell, Pauli and I wandered over to his house. When we got there, I looked toward the top of the huge oak in his front yard. My kite was still stuck up there from last fall.

"I'm getting it," I said.

"No," Pauli said. "That's crazy. It's too high."

"Watch me." I started climbing the oak. I felt fabulous and free. Nothing could hurt me.

"Denjer!"

I looked down as I heard the shout. *Denjer?* I thought.

Pauli's grandma was down below me—far down below, waving a dish towel like a flag and shouting. "Denjer! Denjer!"

Oh. I got it. She was shouting "danger."

"It's okay," I called to her. "I'm safe."

"Bed tings heppen in treeze," she shouted.

"But it's okay," I called back, smiling at the way she'd pronounced the words.

"In treeze! In treeze!" she shouted, pointing to the oak I'd climbed.

Pointing to the oak *tree*, I realized. At that same instant, I heard something start to crack. The branch I was standing on tore from the tree with a splintering scream.

I fell. Also letting out a splintering scream.

I managed to land on Pauli, and that sort of broke my fall. But I still broke my leg. His grandma sure was right. Bad things happen in trees.

THE DEAD WON'T HURT YOU

The gate to the cemetery wasn't locked.

That had been Eric's last hope. He'd been prepared to shake the bars, then turn to his friends and say, "Guess we can't do it."

The gate swung when he pushed, moving without the slightest creak. To Eric, the unexpected silence was worse than any graveyard moan of rusted metal. He felt as if he was watching a movie with the sound turned off. For an instant, he thought of an old, scratchy silent film—that first vampire movie with the freaky-looking bald guy.

"I'm out of here," Bennet said.

Eric made no comment as Bennet raced away. He watched Jacob and Lance, wondering if they'd chicken out, too. They both looked at him, obviously wondering the same thing.

Last chance, Eric thought. All three of them could quit right now, and there'd be no blame anywhere. But the moment came and passed. Eric drew a deep breath of the damp air and stepped through the gate of the cemetery. He checked his watch. Just ten minutes to go. Then, he could leave. He couldn't even remember which of them had suggested they visit a cemetery at midnight.

But once the idea had been spoken, they'd teased and taunted each other until they had to do it. Eric couldn't admit that the cemetery terrified him. Even in daylight—even as far as possible from midnight—he avoided this field of headstones and monuments. Eric thought about last year, when they'd buried Hunter Reynolds. Eric had pretended to be sick so he wouldn't have to go to the funeral and the cemetery. He hadn't even really known Hunter. They weren't in any of the same classes at school. They'd been on that Little League team together three years back, the one that had almost made it to the state playoffs, but that was it.

Eric always kept as much distance as he could between himself and the dead.

Until now.

They walked toward the center of the cemetery, the spot they'd agreed upon for their midnight adventure. Jacob was the next to turn and run. "I can't," he said when they were halfway there. "Sorry."

"Looks like it's just you and me," Lance said.

"Yeah." Eric squeezed out that single word, not trusting his voice to speak a full sentence without trembling. *Not much farther*, he told himself. It wasn't that far to midnight, and it wasn't that far to the center of the cemetery.

Lance stopped walking. "You hear that?"

"No." Eric looked around. "What?"

"I heard something. Footsteps."

"Cut it out." Eric listened to the dead silence around him.

"Man, don't you hear it?" Lance asked.

Eric shook his head.

"Forget this," Lance said. He spun away from Eric and sprinted back toward the gate.

Eric knew he was free to follow his friends. Just being the last to leave—that was a victory. But he was so close. He checked his watch. Only five more minutes.

He continued walking toward the center of the cemetery, his breath growing shallow, his ears straining for any hint of the sounds that had spooked Lance. He heard nothing. Any other place on Earth, the peacefulness would have been pleasant. Here, the silence was a reminder of what lay beneath the ground.

Eric reached the center of the cemetery, then checked his watch. Three minutes. He knew he could make it.

Just this once, he told himself. All he had to do was stay in place and fight the terror for a little while, and he'd be able to do anything—face any fear at all. He looked at the rows of headstones, wondering where Hunter was buried.

"People don't understand."

The voice from behind cut into his thoughts like a hatchet. Eric spun and shouted in surprise.

"Hey, relax," the man said.

"You scared me," Eric said. "I didn't hear you walk up." He was surprised a guy that big could move so quietly.

The man laughed and scraped a foot against the ground.

"I'm not a ghost," he said. He slapped his chest. "See, real and solid."

"Yeah." Eric waited for his nerves to stop buzzing.

The man put a hand on Eric's shoulder. "People don't understand," he said. "There's nothing scary here. The dead won't hurt you."

"Guess not," Eric said. He wanted to pull away.

"No," the man said, "the dead don't hurt anyone. And they keep their secrets."

Eric tried to step back. The fingers tightened on his shoulder.

"It's the living," the man said. "The people who haunt the places where nobody goes. That's who you have to watch out for. It's the people in the alleys, the people in the cemetery at night, the people who hope to catch you alone."

"What?" Eric pulled harder against the man's grip, trying to get free without turning his attempt into a struggle. He didn't understand what this man was talking about. But deep inside, he was afraid he knew exactly what the man meant.

The bell in the town clock began to strike the hour.

The man laughed. He reached toward Eric with his other hand. "Let me go!" Eric shouted. He twisted his body, breaking loose. The instant he slipped from the man's grasp, Eric rushed blindly away.

The man swore and chased after him. Eric could hear the footsteps close behind him. He knew that any second he'd be tackled or grabbed and swept off his feet. Then he'd be found dead like Hunter Reynolds, and the adults would talk about it in whispers.

Eric shouted again, but the bell drowned out his voice. He ran across a stretch of manicured lawn, dodging left and right between headstones, knowing his feet were landing on graves, knowing he stepped on the dead as he raced for his own life.

"Run, boy, run," the man behind him yelled. "Makes it more fun."

The sound of the bell wrapped around Eric like deep water. He gasped, trying to find more speed. As the twelfth peal rode on a wave through the air, Eric heard a scream— short, cut off, a howl of frustration and surprise—followed by another sound that he'd never forget—the wet thud of a thick fruit smashed against a sidewalk.

Eric dared a glance over his shoulder.

He stopped in his tracks. In this field of death, the living man who'd pursued him had—suddenly and undeniably— joined the dead. Trembling, Eric crept back even as his mind screamed for him to keep running.

The man had tripped and fallen, hitting his head on a gravestone. Eric didn't want to look, but he had to. Death was still and quiet and final. The man's legs rested above a grave. The earth was undisturbed except for a spot next to the man's right foot. Here the earth was pushed up, the grass torn, as if a hand had risen to clutch at the passing ankle.

Eric knelt and gently touched the stone. "Thanks," he whispered. He didn't need to read the inscription. He knew who was buried there. "Thanks, Hunter. Sorry I didn't come before."

There was no answer. He expected none. Eric stood and walked slowly toward the cemetery gate. He had no urge to rush. He had no fear. He knew the dead would never hurt him.

COPIES

I hate getting dragged to Dad's office for Take Our Kids to Work Day. It's so boring, I want to scream. But at least I had company this year. My little brother was finally old enough to get dragged along with me.

"You kids are in for a real treat," Dad said when we pulled into the parking lot. "We've upgraded our mail room. And we got a new shredder for the office. Bet you can't wait to see that baby in action, right?"

"Right, Dad," I said, grabbing Nicky by the collar so he wouldn't wander into the path of any of the dozens of cars zipping through the parking lot.

Dad continued listing the wonders that lay ahead of us. "And here's the best part. We just put in two new copiers. Real high-speed top-of-the-line machines. The best money can buy."

Shoot. When he said that, I realized I'd forgotten to bring something to copy. It's fun to run off a couple hundred cartoons and pass them out at school. But I didn't have any-thing with me.

Wait. That wasn't true. I had something way goofier than a cartoon. I had Nicky. The moment we got to Dad's office, I asked if I could check out the copy room.

"Sure," Dad said. "You know the way. Just don't fool around too much. The company has a policy against personal copies."

"You can trust me," I said. "Come on, Nicky, I'll show you Dad's awesome new copiers." I grinned at the thought of how personal a copy could be.

I led Nicky down the hall to the copy room. We were in luck. The place was all ours. "Here," I said, pulling a chair over to one of the copiers. "Get up."

Nicky climbed onto the chair. I lifted the lid of the copier. "Put your face down here," I said. "But close your eyes. It can get real bright."

As always, Nicky did what I told him. I tried to set the machine for ten copies, but my finger slipped. The display showed one thousand. *Hey, why not,* I thought, deciding to leave the number the way it was.

"Here goes." I hit the COPY button.

Man, that sucker was fast. After a couple of seconds, copies started flying out like bullets from a machine gun. They looked real cool. Nicky had his face scrunched up, but you could tell it was him.

I glanced at the second copier and got another idea. I al-most didn't do it, but I couldn't resist. Hey—what's the harm? I slipped down my pants and sat on the machine. I'd heard about kids doing this, but I'd never tried it. I reached over and hit the buttons. Might as well make a thousand copies of my butt to go along with the thousand of Nicky's face.

My machine was even faster. Before I knew it, I'd run off the whole batch. I hopped down and walked back over to Nicky.

"Hey, these aren't that good." I grabbed a copy as it shot out of the machine. The image was kind of faded. I thumbed through the stack. Maybe the machine was running out of supplies. Each copy that came out was a bit more faded.

"Can I get up now?" Nicky asked as the machine hummed to a stop. His voice sounded really muffled.

"Sure. Yeah. It's done."

Nicky stood up.

For a moment, I just stared. Then I blinked.

That was more than Nicky could do. His lips and eyelids were gone. Almost everything was gone. Most of his face had been copied away. Two small holes were all that was left of his nose. A pair of eyes stared out at me from a face like an egg.

Oh man, Dad was going to kick my butt.

My butt!

I raced over to the other machine and grabbed the last copy that came out. Nothing. Just a smooth, round hunk of flesh.

When my hand stopped shaking, I reached down the back of my pants. Smoothness. No crack. Nothing.

Nicky made some kind of noise in his throat, but I

couldn't understand him. Without a mouth, he couldn't talk very clearly.

It was about then that I realized something awful. Truly awful. It was bad enough that Nicky couldn't talk. But I had to go to the bathroom. And without a butt, I couldn't do that, either.

SHAPING THE FOG

There was always fog. The world was never clear. Ken couldn't imagine what it would be like to see into the distance—to gaze far away without the ground and rocks and trees growing fainter and fuzzier and whiter as they blended into the blank sea that formed the edge of the visible world. But there wasn't always good fog.

Today, it looked like good fog.

"Can we?" Serra asked, sneaking up to the window next to Ken.

"I think so," Ken said. He slid aside the screen and touched the air. He frowned for a moment as he rubbed the fog between his fingers, testing the feel. Then he smiled and nodded to Serra.

"Yay!" Serra shouted, leaping into the air.

"Quiet," Ken said. "You'll wake the old man."

"I'll go get Rowen," she whispered.

"Okay. But be quiet." Ken watched Serra tiptoe down the hall.

"Sshhhhh," Ken warned again as Serra herded Rowen along the hallway.

"Good fog?" Rowen asked.

Ken nodded then opened the door slowly, trying to ease it past the spots where the hinges creaked. He followed the others out to the porch. "Not too far," Ken said as they crept down the two steps to the moist ground.

He cupped the fog in his hands and pressed his fingers together. The soft dampness grew firm and warm in his grip. He released the ball and watched as it drifted toward the earth. This was good fog. Ken stooped and placed his hand beneath the piece of fog. He raised it up, stroking it gently, pressing and pushing, pinching, forming until it became a small bird.

"Serra. Catch!" Ken released the bird with a gentle push. It glided from his hand, leaving small wisps of fog behind as it slipped through the material of its creation.

Serra giggled and grabbed the bird. She turned it around and sent it floating back. Ken caught the bird and raised it for a closer look. It had already lost most of its shape. "They never last," he said.

"The old man can make them last," Rowen said, looking up from the large ball he had formed.

"Yeah. It takes practice. Skill, too," Ken said. He reached into the fog again and began to gather another piece.

This time, he made a bat. Serra shrieked as it fluttered toward her, slashing her hands with enough force to turn the creature once more into formless mist.

"Sshhhhh!" Ken said.

"Sorry. You know that scares me." Serra went back to her own sculpting.

Ken stroked the fog and wondered what to make next. He glanced toward Rowen. When he saw what was forming, his heart froze.

"Rowen! No! Never!" Ken rushed forward, waving his hands to create a breeze and puffing hard.

"You ruined it," Rowen said as the fog in front of him dissolved into drifting tendrils.

Ken stood panting, trying to catch his breath. He shook his head. "Don't ever do that again."

"I wanted someone like me," Rowen said. "You and Serra, you're too big. I wanted someone small."

"If he'd seen . . ." Ken said. "He's told us a thousand times. Never like us. Never make our own form."

"They do not last." The voice, soft and sad, drifted from the porch. "Or if they last, they do not obey," the old man said, walking stiffly down the steps.

Ken tried to explain. "He didn't mean to. He didn't know. He's young. It won't happen again."

"No," the old man said. "It won't." He took a deep breath and gently puffed the air toward Rowen. The boy swirled back into the fog from which he'd been formed. Another breath, and Serra was gone. He took a third breath and faced Ken.

Ken felt himself fading. As his awareness bled into the waiting mist, he saw the old man reach out and gently scoop a handful of fog.

WILLARD'S OPPOSITIONAL NOTEBOOK

On the very day that Willard decided to organize his life, he found a small notebook at a neighborhood garage sale. *Perfect*, Willard thought as he picked up the spiral-bound memo pad. "How much?" he asked the woman who stood in the driveway next to a pile of musty clothes, rusty tools, and dusty romance novels.

"Quarter," she said.

Willard knew people expected customers to bargain at a garage sale, so he said, "I'll give you a dime."

"Sold," the woman said.

"Okay," Willard said when he got home. "Now I can list everything I want to do." He grabbed a pen from the kitchen counter and wrote the first three things that came to mind: *clean my room, finish my book report, watch* Cartoon Cavalcade *at six tonight.*

"Whatcha got?" his sister Tammy asked as Willard was closing the notebook.

"Nothing," Willard said.

"Can I see?"

"Nope." He put the notebook in his pocket and started up to his room.

Before he got halfway up the stairs, the phone rang. It was his friend Preston. "I got my new video game," Preston said. "Want to come check it out?"

"Sure." Willard rushed over.

He stayed at Preston's until dinnertime.

It wasn't until the next morning that Willard realized he hadn't done anything on his list. He ripped out the page and threw it away. Then he tried again.

"What are you writing?" Tammy asked as Willard made a note to put air in his bicycle tires.

"None of your business," Willard said.

"Can I write something?" she asked.

Willard glared at his sister. "You don't know how to write."

"I can write my name," Tammy told him. "I'll show you."

"Leave me alone." Willard went outside to get away from his sister.

The next day, when Willard got on his bike and saw how squishy the tires were, he realized he'd forgotten about the air.

After several weeks of similar experiences, it began to dawn on Willard that anything he wrote failed to happen. From there, Willard made a small leap to a great idea. His hand trembled as he wrote the note to himself. *Fail my math test.*

Willard scored a B on the test, without even trying.

During the next month, Willard got great grades and wonderful gifts. The school bully left town. The movie theater let him in for free. He went to a ton of birthday parties. In every way possible, life was fabulous.

But paper was running out.

Willard held the notebook in his hands and thought about what he should write on the final page. He didn't want to waste it.

Then he got the best idea of all. He wrote one word. Three small letters. *Die.* That was all.

This time, Willard wasn't going to rip the page out. He planned to leave it bound forever between the covers. But he needed to put it somewhere safe. Somewhere it would never be disturbed. Willard left the notebook on his bed and went out the front door to check. Great—they were pouring concrete for the foundation of a new house down the block.

Willard searched in the basement until he found a small metal box. Then he went to his room. "Hey, what are you doing?" he asked Tammy, who was standing by Willard's bedroom door.

"Nothing," she said. She giggled and ran down the hall.

Willard hurried into his room and shoved the notebook in the box before his nosey sister could come back to snoop, then wrapped tape around it. That evening, right after the workers left, Willard snuck over to the site and pushed the box beneath the concrete.

Forever. Willard felt great. He went home and celebrated by making himself a hot fudge sundae. It didn't spoil his appetite.

For the next month, Willard felt absolutely wonderful. The secret was so fabulous, he almost spilled it to his friends. But he wanted to keep it to himself for a while.

As great as he felt, he also felt hungry. Willard gained twelve pounds that month. *Can't hurt me*, he told himself. *I'm never going to die.*

The next month, Willard gained eighteen pounds. As he stood looking at himself in a mirror in his room, Willard realized he had to watch what he ate. But at the moment he thought about it, another thought struck him—a thought that made him race down the hall to Tammy's room.

"You wrote in it, didn't you?" he asked.

Tammy shook her head.

"Tell the truth, Tammy. This is no joke. I know what you wrote," Willard said, feeling the warm sweat of fear flowing down his forehead and the back of his neck.

"Just one letter," she said. "That's all. I wanted to show you I could write my name. I started to. But then I heard you coming and got scared you'd yell at me."

In his mind, Willard saw the page from the notebook. With *die*, followed by the start of Tammy's name. Just one letter. Enough to turn *die* into *diet*.

Willard wanted to scream at his sister, but that could wait. At the moment, he had an irresistible urge. There was a huge hunk of chocolate cake in the fridge, and it was calling to him.

A TINY LITTLE PIECE

Julie couldn't wait to get to the museum. All week, she'd been looking forward to the trip. The museum had a special new exhibit—an actual mummy. It was part of an amazing discovery that had been made last year in Egypt. Julie had heard all about it on the news, and later she'd watched a special on one of the science channels. Archaeologists had uncovered an enormous tomb containing two thousand mummies, all perfectly preserved. The mummies had been sent to exhibitions throughout the world. And Julie was going to get to see one today—right in Grandville at the Junior Museum.

"I'll bet it's real gross," her friend Tina said as they got off the bus.

"I think it'll be cool," Julie said. "Come on." She hurried to the front of the group.

"What's the rush?" Tina asked, trailing along behind her. "The mummy's been around for thousands of years. It isn't going anywhere."

"I just can't wait," Julie said. But she figured she'd be disappointed with the display. Her mom had taken her to lots of museums, and the good stuff was always inside glass cases or roped off so nobody could get close.

This time, it was different. Julie gasped as she rushed from the entrance into the main exhibit hall of the museum. There it was—right on a table. No ropes, no bars. It was in a case, but the lid was open.

"Aren't they supposed to be kept sealed?" Tina asked.

"Yeah." Julie pushed forward with the rest of her class. She walked right up to the mummy and leaned over the case. She jerked back as she saw her hair almost fall across the bandaged body. The long, blond hair she was so proud of made a strange contrast where it dangled next to the dead gray wrappings.

"I told you it was gross," Tina said from behind her.

"No, it isn't," Julie said.

"Then touch it," Tina told her.

Julie was about to say *No way!* But she paused and thought about it. *Why not?* She might never get another chance. As she snuck one hand over the edge of the case, she braced herself, waiting for someone to shout, but nobody in the crowd of students was looking at her. Others were reaching out toward the mummy, but none of them had dared touch it yet.

Julie put a hand on the ancient shoulder. The bandages felt dry and crackly, like fallen leaves. Beneath her fingers, she felt a bit of loose fabric. Checking again to make sure nobody was watching, Julie pulled at the flaked edge. *Mine,* she thought. *My own piece of history.* With the tiniest whisper of a rip, the fragment of bandage came free. Julie clutched it in her fist, not believing her luck.

"Kids, line up over there," the teacher said. "I don't think we're supposed to be this close. Mr. Desmond from the museum will be here in a moment to tell us all about the mummy."

Julie backed away from the mummy and joined her classmates along the side wall. A moment later, a man came through a doorway on the other side of the room. He put a piece of paper inside the case next to the mummy's leg, and then closed the lid.

Julie saw there was a number on the paper. This was mummy three hundred forty-seven. She suspected that Mr. Desmond had never taken care of a mummy before.

"We're very lucky," he said. "A museum this small rarely gets to have such an exhibit. It's quite a treasure." He paused and looked toward the mummy, then started talking again. "We've lost so much of the past. A little here, a little there. So much is gone."

For an instant, Julie felt guilty. The piece of bandage seemed to dissolve in her palm. She opened her fingers a tiny crack and peeked down. The souvenir was still there, lying dead and gray against the flesh of her palm. Julie thought about what the man had said. If every person took a small piece, there'd be no mummy left. She considered returning the fragment, but there was no way she could repair the damage. It was torn off, and that was that.

No big deal.

The class was allowed to step up to the case after Mr. Desmond finished his talk. Julie took a quick look, but something about the mummy made her uneasy now.

"I told you it was gross," Tina said as they left the building. She shuddered.

Julie didn't say anything.

When she got home, she looked for a place to keep the piece of bandage. She didn't want to shove it in her drawer—it would get lost or crushed. And she didn't want to leave it out, where her mom might mistake it for a worthless scrap of garbage and throw it away. She had several boxes on her dresser. One was for jewelry, another for her hair bands and ribbons, and a third was for letters and cards. Finally, she decided to put the piece in her jewelry box.

"My own little piece of history," she said as she closed the lid. She was over the guilt now, and glad she'd taken the treasure. She felt good about it all day long, and all that evening.

The mummy came in the night.

His dry wrapped feet made barely a sound on the floor. His body produced light crackles like the thin plastic on a box of candy.

Julie made a sound of her own as she sat up in bed and stared at the mummy standing in her doorway—but that sound caught in her throat and came out as little more than a hiss.

The mummy crossed the room, moving stiffly on knees that hardly bent. He reached toward Julie.

"Here," Julie said. She grabbed for her jewelry box. "Take it. Take all of it. Those are all my treasures."

The mummy's hand moved toward her head.

Julie fumbled in the box, spilling earrings, bracelets, and necklaces in a tangle on her lap. She fumbled for the piece of bandage and finally managed to grip it in fingers that felt numb and useless.

"Take it," she begged, holding up the fragment.

The mummy's hand jerked back from Julie's head. She felt a small, sharp pain in her scalp.

Julie saw a hair dangling from the bandaged fingers—one thin strand of hair. That was all. The mummy turned. As he dragged his ancient body back across the room, Julie's eyes settled on the tag attached to his leg. Mummy number three hundred forty-seven.

She sighed in relief as the mummy left, then carefully rubbed her head where the hair had been plucked. It could have been worse, she realized. But the mummy had taken only one tiny little piece. That seemed like a fair trade. A piece of hair for a piece of bandage.

"One little piece can't hurt," Julie said as she closed her eyes and tried to sleep. She was still trembling, but she knew it was over. She'd never see that mummy again. He had his piece.

Mummy number seventy-nine came the next night. He yanked a hair from her head. Just one small piece.

The night after that, it was mummy number four hundred eighty-six.

Just one little piece.

Julie shuddered as she thought about those words. *Just one little piece.*

Just two thousand mummies. Two thousand hairs. Two thousand visits in the middle of the night. Julie felt she was losing it—her hair, her mind—one little piece at a time.

THE LA BREA TOY PITS

We have arrived!" Lyle's father announced, waking Lyle from his nap.

"We're here, we're here, we're here!" Lyle's little brother Scotty shouted. "Yay!"

"Chill out, Scotty," Lyle said as he sat up and stretched. "It's just a bunch of pits full of gooky stuff." He didn't know why his folks had dragged them there. He'd seen the place on TV, and there was nothing exciting about it. So what if some dinosaurs had been stupid enough to get stuck in the tar a zillion years ago?

"Are you sure this is it?" Lyle's mom asked. She pointed out the window. "That seems like a small sign for such a famous place."

Lyle looked. The sign didn't offer much information, except that this was the way to The Pits. There was an arrow at the bottom, aimed at a path that curved out of sight to the left.

"Certainly," Lyle's dad said. He patted the map that was lying on the dashboard. "I always know where I'm going."

"It looks a lot smaller than I expected," Lyle's mom said. "And there aren't any other cars."

"Stop worrying," his dad said. "This is the right place. We just got here ahead of the rush."

"If you say so. Come on, kids," Lyle's mom said. "Let's go."

Lyle grabbed his yo-yo and followed the family through the empty parking lot. "I need a new string," he called to his mom.

"Lyle, stop fooling around with that thing and pay attention," his mom said. "We didn't drive all the way here so you could play."

"That's for sure," Lyle muttered. He checked out his yo-yo string. It was worn pretty badly in a couple of spots but, with luck, it would last for a few more days. He wound it up and did an around-the-world.

Ploink!

Lyle reached out as the string broke and his yo-yo went flying through the air. It bounced to a landing and clattered across the solid tar of the parking lot, wobbling like a small animal that had just run headfirst into a large tree.

"My yo-yo!" he said, chasing off after it.

The yo-yo rolled down a hill at the edge of the parking lot. Lyle glanced at his parents. "I'll be right there," he called.

"Don't get lost," his mom called back. "We'll meet you at the tar pits." She and the others headed for the path that led from the parking lot through a field.

46

Lyle chugged down the hill. When he reached the bottom, he stared at the strange landscape. It took him a moment to realize what he was looking at. The first toy that caught his eye barely looked like a toy. He stared at the strangely familiar object for long seconds before the shape made sense to his mind.

"A tricycle," he said. Half sunk in the ground, the discarded vehicle was mostly dull brown and black from rust and weather.

It took Lyle another second to realize that the whole area in front of him was filled with toys—heaps and piles of toys. Most of them were in far better shape than the tricycle, and far more interesting. Many even looked brand-new.

"Wow," Lyle whispered, forgetting about his yo-yo. Stretching before him was every toy he'd ever dreamed of, and many he never knew existed.

Lyle stepped on the seat of the tricycle. It wobbled a little, but it didn't tip. Right past the handlebars, Lyle saw a model of the SR-71 Blackhawk. He reached down and pulled it free from the muck. "Cool," he said. He took another step, planting his foot on an official NBA basketball that was three-quarters submerged in the muck. Just ahead, he saw a radio-controlled car—the kind with the really large tires and directional steering. "Awesome," Lyle said. He dropped the plane and picked up the car.

The controller was only a few feet away, wedged between a red Radio Flyer wagon and a pogo stick. Lyle stepped on a Cabbage Patch doll and grinned as he felt the head sink down.

Lyle's grin faded as his foot kept sinking.

"Hey . . ." He staggered, setting his other foot down hard against the top of a Chutes and Ladders board. The board tilted and sunk into the tar. Small bubbles rose to the goopy surface and burst. Lyle's foot sank in right after the board.

"Oh man," Lyle said. He tried to pull his foot out.

No use.

"Help!" Lyle cried. "I'm stuck!"

There was no answer.

"HELP!" Lyle cried again, as loudly as he could.

"Lyle," his mom called from far off.

"Over here!" Lyle shouted. He felt himself sinking deeper. "Hurry. I'm stuck."

"Good grief, Lyle," his dad called from behind him. "How did you get yourself in such a mess?"

Lyle heard his dad scrambling over the toys. Then he felt a strong pair of hands grab his sides and pull. His dad lifted him from the tar.

"Look at your pants, young man," his mom said when Lyle had been deposited on solid turf. "Maybe this will teach you not to run off."

"Oh, I think he's learned his lesson," Lyle's dad said. "Haven't you, son?"

"Yeah," Lyle said. "I sure have."

His dad grinned and ruffled Lyle's hair. "How about we go see those tar pits? Okay, son?"

"Sure, Dad," Lyle said. "That sounds great." He followed his parents away from the toys.

"I think we can cut through here," his dad said, angling to

the left at the bottom of the hill. They walked a short dis-tance through thick weeds.

Lyle's mom saw it first. "Oh my word, look at that dining room set," she said. Carrying Scotty, she dashed ahead of the others.

Lyle's father gasped. "A metric socket wrench. Isn't that a beauty." He rushed forward.

"Toasters," his mom said. "All those toasters. My word—there's a four-slice model."

Lyle chased after his parents, but they were already deep into the pile of Thighmasters, DVD players, Civil War chess sets, and power tools. "Stop," Lyle shouted, stepping on top of an outdoor gas grill. The grill shifted and sank deeper into the tar.

"Look, hon," Lyle's dad called to Lyle's mom, holding up a chrome showerhead. "Wouldn't this be great in the bath-room? It has five different spray settings, plus a water-saver option and a heavy-duty pulsing mode."

"Dishes," his mom exclaimed, bending down to stroke the fine china at her feet. "What a lovely pattern." She sank lower, taking Scotty with her.

Lyle leaped from the grill, aiming for the top of a surround-sound stereo speaker. He missed and came down into a puddle of muck between a garage-door opener and a Weed Whacker. "Mom!" he shouted. "Dad!"

They didn't seem to hear him. Lyle sighed. Lyle sank. He looked at his parents. They were sinking, too, but they didn't appear to mind. Scotty minded. But, as usual, nobody was paying attention to him.

Lyle sank to his chest and then to his chin. As the tar reached his ears, he heard his last words.

It was his mom speaking. "A pasta maker," she said. "I'd give anything for one of those."

MR. LAMBINI'S HAUNTED HOUSE

are you."

"Dare *you*."

"I'll go if you go."

"You're scared."

"No, I'm not."

"Are, too."

And so, daring each other and teasing each other, Cindy and her friend Beth walked up the path that led to Mr. Lambini's house.

All evening, they'd met kids who'd been there. Everyone was talking about how great and scary it was. Cindy looked at the large piece of wood leaning against the willow tree in Mr. Lambini's front yard. Two dripping words were painted in bloodred letters on a black background: HAUNTED HOUSE.

"I'm not scared of anything," Cindy said. And she wasn't. She'd yet to meet an experience she couldn't handle. Movies, books, even creepy rides—none of it bothered Cindy.

She led the way to Mr. Lambini's porch. *Not bad*, she thought as she studied the scarecrow in the front yard. It looked like it was rigged to move. Sure enough, as she walked past, the arm swung out and a tape-recorded voice said, "Boooohhhooooohhooooohoooo!"

Cindy wasn't scared.

But Beth jumped half a mile, nearly leaving her shoes behind.

"Scared?" Cindy asked Beth when she came back down.

"Nah," Beth said, with just the faintest tremble in her voice. "Just startled."

Cindy smiled. The scarecrow was a good sign. They never put the scariest stuff by the entrance. They always saved the good stuff for inside. So, if the entrance was this scary, the rest of the haunted house should be great.

They walked up to the porch. Three other kids—a small cowboy and two hockey players—were standing there, as if trying to build up the courage to ring the bell. Cindy recognized them easily enough despite their costumes. It was Dwayne, Brian, and Brian's little brother, Tim. She smiled and walked past them. "What were you waiting for?" she asked as she rang the bell.

The door swung open. "Enter," a deep, booming voice said.

Cindy paused, bracing herself for anything that might jump at her. Nothing popped up, so she stepped inside. The walls were draped with sheets, leaving a corridor for them to walk through. Opposite where she stood, a sign said EN-TRANCE. Below the word, there was an arrow pointing to the right.

"Cool," Cindy said, turning toward the right. "Maybe we'll go through the whole house."

"But we don't really know him," Beth said.

Cindy realized Beth was right. She knew the man's name, but nothing else about him. Still, she wasn't going to turn back. Cindy wasn't scared. "Lots of kids have been here. There's nothing to worry about." She headed down the hall.

Cindy hadn't gone more than ten steps when the vampire jumped out from behind a sheet.

"Mwwwwaahhaaaahhaahhaaa!" he screamed. Then he vanished behind the walls.

Cindy wasn't scared. But she had to admit the vampire makeup was pretty good.

Beth gasped, but she stayed next to Cindy, clutching her arm so hard Cindy was sure there'd be a bruise the next morning.

Little Tim wailed like a banshee and ran off, his cowboy hat flying from his head as he galloped for safety. Brian chased after him.

Cindy went farther into the house.

The headless man popped out of nowhere and swung an ax at her. Even in the gloom of the narrow corridor, she could see the blade was rubber.

Sure enough, it bounced off her.

Cindy glanced back when she realized nobody was grabbing her arm. "Beth, hold on," she called, but it was too late. She caught a last glimpse of Beth as her friend vanished around the corner, heading back the way they'd come.

Dwayne was still there—until the skull came flying at them, hissing like a snake, sparks flying from its eyes.

Dwayne made tracks for the door. Cindy watched the skull swing back and forth on the piece of fishing line. "Pretty cool," she said.

Cindy wasn't scared, not even when the bats dropped from above. Not even when the man with the chainsaw leaped out of the darkness, or when the grasping hands burst through the walls on either side of her, their nails dark with fresh-turned earth.

She came, at last, to the end of the tour. "Well done," a man said. "Nobody else has been this brave." He reached into a plastic pumpkin on a table next to him and handed her a candy bar. "Oh, take two. I've got plenty." He handed her a second one.

"Thanks," Cindy said. She thought about giving one to Beth, but Beth hadn't earned it. Beth had been scared. "This isn't bad," Cindy added as the man opened a door for her. She stepped through the doorway, but still looked back at the man. There was something else she wanted to tell him. "It wasn't scary, but I wasn't expecting all that much from someone's homemade haunted house."

"Oh, this is just the entrance," the man said. "The haunted house is on the other side." He smiled and closed the door.

Cindy turned around and looked. The walls on either side of her were old and rotting. The floor was thick with dust. In the darkness ahead, something shuffled and stirred, waiting for her.

Cindy listened.

Chains rattled. Bits of dry flesh fell from bones and hit the floor with muffled thumps. Fangs smacked together in anticipation. Creatures howled.

Cindy wasn't scared. Not now. This time, Cindy was terrified.

NUMBSKULL

omeone hasn't been brushing," Dr. Peterson told me as he examined my X ray.

"I brush," I said. I looked at the X ray, too, trying to figure out what it was that he was seeing.

That's when he said those words. Up until then, I'd never heard them directed at me, though I'd feared them. It was like hearing a jury say "Guilty." He opened his mouth and told me, "You have a cavity."

I felt my stomach try to leap out past my throat. My lungs went flat and fluttered like deflated balloons. My intestines started dancing. "A cavity?" Maybe I'd misheard him. Maybe he'd asked me if I had a canary. Maybe he asked if I had a favorite charity.

Dr. Peterson nodded. "Yes, a cavity. Fortunately for you, I had a cancellation. You won't have to wait. We can take care of it right now."

"Uh, maybe I should come back . . ."

"Michael," he said, "it's best to get it over with. It's not that bad. Honest. Now, you have a choice. If you don't like needles, I can just drill the cavity. That will hurt a little. Or I can give you a shot. The shot will hurt for a tiny bit, but then you won't feel any pain when I drill."

What a choice. "No shot," I said. But as the words left my lips, I thought about sitting there while he dug inside my mouth with a power tool. The idea of him making a hole in my tooth was more than I wanted to deal with. "Wait, I'll take the shot."

"You sure?"

I nodded. I almost changed my mind when I saw the size of the needle. It looked like something my mom would use to put icing on cookies. The needle got bigger and bigger as he brought it near me. Then it turned fuzzy as it got too close for my eyes to focus on. When he gave me the shot, it stung for a second. But once it was over, I had to admit the experience wasn't as bad as I'd thought it would be.

In a few minutes, my mouth was numb. Not long after that, Dr. Peterson had drilled and filled my cavity.

"All set," he told me after I'd done one final rinse and spit. "But be careful for the next hour or two. Your mouth is going to be numb. Watch your tongue. Be careful you don't bite it."

"Okay." I climbed out of the chair. One side of my mouth was totally numb. My tongue didn't have any feeling, either. I wondered if I was drooling.

"Not too bad, right?" Dr. Peterson said as I left the room.

"For you," I said. "What else do you do for fun—stomp on baby animals?"

Yikes. I don't know why I'd said that. Dr. Peterson just

stood there with his mouth open—which was a switch since it's usually not the dentist who has his mouth open. I turned away from him and left the office. I hoped he wasn't the sort to hold a grudge. I didn't want him angry with me the next time he started poking around inside my mouth with those sharp tools.

But I was happy to be outside and free. Mom had dropped me off on her way to the store, and I had to walk home. It wasn't far. I hadn't gone more than half a block when this guy came up to me and asked if I knew where Thurston Street was.

"What do I look like? A tour guide?" I clamped my jaw shut, not believing what had come out of my mouth.

"Well, aren't you a rude little brat," the man said before he walked off.

I had this sudden fear that I'd bitten my tongue and didn't even know it. That thought was enough to make me unclamp my teeth. I touched my tongue, then looked at my finger. There was no blood. That was good.

But something was wrong. I was saying stuff I never would have dreamed of saying. I couldn't control my tongue. It had to be the shot. I knew I'd be fine as soon as it wore off. Yeah, that's all I had to do—wait until the numbness was gone. After that, everything would be okay. And if I was ever unlucky enough to need another filling, I'd just skip the needle.

A couple of hours—that's what Dr. Peterson had said. I'd just go home and stay inside until then.

"Hey, snothead, what's new?"

I looked up—right into a ton of trouble. Standing just two feet from me was Smasher Dolenze, the meanest bully in the school. The safest answer was something wimpy like, "Nothing. What's new with you?" But I didn't trust my tongue. I clamped my teeth shut.

"What's the matter, nerd boy? Got nothing to say?"

I shook my head and clamped my jaw down even harder. I could feel the muscles in my neck straining.

Smasher took a step closer to me. Now he was right in my face. "What's wrong? Think you're too good to talk to me?" He pushed me on the shoulder.

I stepped back a step. He followed. "Is that it? Think you're too good?"

I shook my head again and tried to look innocent. Smasher jabbed his fingers into my stomach.

He didn't jab me hard, but it was enough to make me open my mouth. Once my mouth was open, it was all over. "You pathetic loser. You worthless bullying piece of garbage. You aren't even fit to be seen with real humans." It was all spilling out and I couldn't stop it. "You low-life slime-faced monkey brain. I've seen better things than you on the bottom of my shoes. I've seen—"

I couldn't stop it, but Smasher could. I saw the punch flying toward me at ninety miles an hour. Then everything went black.

For a moment, when I woke up, I had no idea where I was. Someone was in my face. I tried to get away.

"Easy, there. Take it easy. Everything's all right."

I recognized the voice. It was Dr. Peterson.

"What happened?" My mouth hurt when I spoke. I must have been unconscious for a while. I could feel again. The novocaine was wearing off.

"You're a lucky boy," Dr. Peterson said. "Somebody found you and brought you in here. The damage isn't too bad. Everything can be fixed."

"I'll be okay?"

"Certainly. The bad news is that you'll have to make five or six visits. There's a lot of repair work for me to do. But there's good news, too."

"What's that?" I asked.

"Well, we already know you aren't afraid of a little needle. And that's a good thing. The work I have to do would be very painful without novocaine. But lucky you, you don't seem to have any problem getting a shot. That's pretty good news, wouldn't you say?"

I nodded, but I really didn't know what to say. Worse, I really didn't know what I'd be saying later, either.

A LITTLE NIGHT FISHING

Wally Klein was a fishing nut. All us kids fished a bit—some more than others—but no one came close to Wally. He lived and breathed fishing the way other kids lived and breathed basketball or music or food. As much as he loved fishing, Wally never talked you to death on the subject. But if a kid came up to Wally and said, "My dad's taking me up north for pike. What's a good lure?" then Wally would talk for as long as anyone wanted to listen on the subject of pike lures or jigging techniques, or just about anything connected to fishing.

So I wasn't really surprised when he walked over to me on the playground and asked, "Want to go fishing?"

I'd fished with him once in a while. It was fun. He seemed happy whether he caught fish or I caught fish, or even if we were just fishing and didn't catch anything. "Where?" I asked.

"New spot. Out past the old abbey."

Wally was always looking for new places to fish. I remember seeing a bunch of maps scattered on the floor of his room the last time I was there. The old abbey hadn't been used for years. I think it belonged to a bunch of monks ages ago. "Sounds good. What time?"

"Seven."

"Isn't that a bit late? It'll be dark by eight."

"Night fishing. You'll like it."

"Okay, I'll meet you in front of the school."

"Good." Wally nodded and took off.

I'd never gone night fishing. It sounded like fun. I hung around the playground for a while and shot some more hoops, then went home to get my stuff ready. I had a rod and reel my uncle had given me a few years back. It was a pretty good setup. And I had my own tackle box, crammed full of stuff I'd picked up over the years.

I thought my folks might stop me from going out at night, but Dad just said, "Wish I could join you," and Mom said, "Have a nice time, dear."

Wally was waiting for me at the school. "Here," he said, handing me a small cooler. "You take this, and I'll take the rods."

"Crawlers?" I asked.

He nodded. "And a couple of sodas."

"Great. Is night fishing any different?" I asked.

"Not much. You can't see your line very well so you have to go by feel. The fish will hear the bait hit, then find it by smell, so there's no problem there." He went on, giving me a mini-education in the art of night fishing as we walked up the hill to the old abbey.

We went past the building, then turned down a small path that led to some woods. "This way," Wally said, disappearing among the trees.

"Wait up." The setting sun cast just enough light so I could see him ahead of me. We walked for ten or fifteen minutes, then broke into a clearing near a large pond. I could just make out the opposite bank, maybe fifty yards away.

"I'd guess it's about six acres," Wally said, anticipating my question. "There's a whole world under that water—a whole world we aren't part of." Wally almost sounded sad when he said that. I passed him the cooler. He pulled out two containers of night crawlers, put one in the pocket of his fishing vest, and gave the other one to me.

I pried up the lid and grabbed a crawler, then baited my hook with the large, plump worm. I lost sight of my bait as the cast went out, then heard a splash in the distance when the worm hit the water. I got a nibble almost immediately. Moments later, I had my first fish—a largemouth bass. "Nice spot," I said to Wally as I unhooked the bass and put it back in the water.

"I think it's special here," he said.

"What do you mean?"

"I'm not sure. It's like something is calling to me. I feel like I belong here."

I had no idea what he meant. I went back to fishing. We both caught a lot of bass at first. And some catfish. The action lasted for about an hour. I hooked something real strong, but my line broke. Then things died down. We didn't get a bite for a long time.

"Ready to quit?" I asked.

"Not yet. I think I'm getting a nibble." He said nothing for a moment, then shouted, "Whoa, big hit!"

I watched his rod bend. Wally held on with two hands. Something had grabbed his bait, something that had no plans to come in without a fight. Wally took a step forward, his foot just touching the edge of the water. He pulled back on the rod, then reeled in as he lowered the tip, gaining a bit of line. But he soon lost what he'd gained when the line started feeding out again.

"This is the one," he said. "This is the fish I've been waiting for all my life."

It was weird. The line wasn't ripping out fast like there was a fish trying to get away—it was spooling out slowly. Wally fought back, bringing in more line. He took another step forward. His whole right foot was in the water now, up to the ankle. I didn't think he noticed.

"Wally, you're getting wet."

He paid no attention. He just held on to the rod, cranked a bit, then stepped forward again.

Both feet were in the water.

"Wally, you're going to ruin those shoes." It sounded pretty stupid, but I had no idea what to say to get through to him. "Come on, Wally, let it go."

He stepped forward. The water was almost up to his right knee.

"Wally!" I tried to pry the rod from his hands. His fingers were locked so hard I couldn't move them at all. Whatever was on the other end of that line, I could feel its strength through the rod. It scared me enough to make me let go and back off.

Wally mumbled something. I wasn't sure what he said, but it sounded like, "It wants me."

I ran for my tackle box. I threw the lid open and fumbled for my knife. Wally might kill me for doing it, but I was going to cut the line. A sharp sting shot through my hand. One of my lures snagged my palm. I yanked the hook out, ignored the pain, and kept looking. There—I found the knife. The stupid blade was rusted stuck. After breaking the nail on my index finger, I finally got the knife open. I turned back to Wally.

He was gone.

A ripple spread across the water in the moonlight. I didn't even think. I just jumped in and tried to follow the muddy bottom of the pond. The water made the blackness complete. I couldn't see anything. I could only feel around. Over and over, dive, swim, breathe, dive again. . . . Nothing. I finally crawled out and collapsed on the bank.

As soon as I got my breath back, I ran toward town. The closest place I could stop for help was the fire station. They organized a search. Everyone tried their best. All they ever found was his rod. There was no line left on the reel.

I stayed away for a month, but I knew I had to go back. And I knew it had to be at night. I stood by the water, thinking about what had happened. There's only one way I can explain it to myself. While Wally was fishing for bass, something down there was fishing for Wally. And, just like Wally wasn't mean or evil, maybe whatever got him wasn't mean or evil, either. Maybe he was caught because he belonged down there. I was thinking about this, and wondering whether it was a crazy idea, when I saw him.

At first, I thought it was a trick of the moonlight, but then I knew it was real. He was under the water, looking up, pressing his hands against the surface like it was glass or a mirror. He opened his mouth and spoke.

No sound came out, but I could tell what he was saying. "Join me."

I almost ran. But in my heart, I knew that if I ran, I'd be running for the rest of my life. So I waited. It might have been minutes. It might have been hours. Time didn't exist on the water that night. I waited until Wally sank back down. Or maybe he faded. I'm not sure which it was. Either way, he was gone. I stood there until the sun began to rise above the woods, thinking about Wally. I thought about Wally, and fishing, and life. Then I left.

I fish a lot now. I guess it's my way of keeping his memory alive. Sometimes, when I'm near water, I still hear him calling.

PRECIOUS MEMORIES

Dad's going to kill me. I can't believe I did it. It was so stupid. But it was an accident. I was running out of the house, late for basketball practice, when I remembered that they were showing *Frankenstein* on cable. So I threw in a tape and set the VCR. It wasn't until I got home and checked the tape that I saw what I'd done. I could feel all the blood drain from my skin as I held the tape in my hand and read the label—YELLOWSTONE NATIONAL PARK, SUMMER VACATION, followed by the date.

I'd just taped over one of Dad's vacation videos. This was serious. Dad spent just about every minute of our vacations with the video camera in his hands. He'd gotten the camera before I was born. I think he was the only parent in the neighborhood who hadn't gone digital. It was a big old thing, and he lugged it everywhere we went. It was almost like he didn't even know whether he'd had a fun vacation until he looked at the videos. Nothing was real for him until he saw it on television.

And now I'd wiped out Yellowstone Park.

There was no way I could hide it from him. He looked at the tapes all the time. He was always going through them and making special tapes by combining clips from lots of vacations. He'd been working on a state park tape for a couple weeks. He didn't even do it on the computer. He used a couple VCRs he'd hooked together.

My best chance was to tell him the news when he was in a good mood. Mom was making lasagna tonight, so I figured Dad would be stuffed and happy after dinner.

"Dad, I had an accident," I told him as he burped and pushed his plate away.

"What kind of accident, Ricky?" he asked, glancing toward me like he was about to go to sleep.

"One of your tapes . . ."

His eyes shot open. "Which tape?"

"Yellowstone," I said, my voice dropping to just above a whisper.

"Yellowstone?" Dad frowned. "I'd love to go there some day. But I don't have any tapes of it."

"But we went there back in . . ." I stopped and tried to remember. I could have sworn we'd been there, but now I couldn't find a single memory.

"Help your mother with the dishes," Dad said.

"Sure." I might have been puzzled, but more than that, I was relieved. I wasn't going to get punished.

The next day, I erased Williamsburg. I'd had a rotten time on that vacation. I had some sort of stomach virus. All I wanted to do was throw up, and Mom kept dragging me around to look at candle makers and all this other colonial stuff.

As soon as I started recording over the tape, the memory began to fade. It was as if the bad experience had never happened.

"Dad?" I asked at dinner that night.

"Yes?"

"Have you ever wanted to go to Williamsburg?"

Dad nodded. "I'd love to go there some time. Maybe we can fit it in next year. What do you think?"

"Sounds great." As I finished my meal, I started searching my mind for my worst memories. It didn't take long to come up with the next candidate.

In third grade, I'd been forced to be an owl in our class play. I don't like talking in front of other people. Especially when I had to end each sentence with, "Whooo, whooo." Even worse, I had to do my talking in an owl costume Mom made. And costumes are not Mom's best thing. I looked like a combination of a feather duster and something that had been run over in the road.

I forgot my lines. I tripped walking onto the stage. And Tara Keller pushed me real hard as we were walking off.

Dad had it all on tape. He was so proud of it, he played it for all the relatives every Thanksgiving.

I didn't even bother to wait until Dad was at work. I went and found the tape labeled RICKY—SCHOOL PLAY and popped it into the VCR. I pressed record and sat back, knowing that the worst experience in my life was about to become less than a memory.

"Has anyone seen a tape labeled SCHOOL PLAY?" Dad called from the next room.

I froze for an instant, but then relaxed. It didn't matter. Even if he was looking for it, he'd forget all about it once I taped over it. He couldn't look for something that he'd forgotten about.

"Haven't seen it," I said.

Dad walked in and shook his head. "I have to find it. It's not just the play. I was putting together a special tape. It's all about you. It starts with the video I made when you were born. I was right there in the hospital with my camera."

I dove for the VCR and jabbed my finger at the STOP button.

"That's odd," the man said. "Who left the VCR on?" He looked around the empty living room.

"What did you say?" his wife asked from the kitchen.

"Nothing." The man turned off the recorder, then went back to reading his newspaper. Sometimes, he wondered whether he should buy a video camera, but without any kids to take pictures of, there didn't seem to be much point in getting one.

BABY TALK

Being the older sister was not a job I would have picked if I'd been given a choice. I had to walk the dog, change the cat litter, clean the fishbowl, and help with the chores, while my baby brother got to lie around drinking milk, chewing cookies, and basically doing nothing useful. Chuck was six months old. I mean, he was sort of cute, and babies can be fun, but he got all the attention while I got all the work.

He certainly got all of my attention the first time he talked. I was walking past his crib when he looked up at me with that toothless, wet grin and said, "Hey, sis, what's new?"

I was a bit less articulate with my reply. I think I said, "Huh?"

Chuck bounced and squealed a bit, then said, "Relax—you look like you just saw a ghost."

I managed to reply with a full sentence. "You can talk."

Chuck shrugged. "That appears to be the case."

I suddenly saw my whole future flash past my eyes. I'd be the sister of the amazing talking baby. No one would ever know anything else about me. Chuck would become famous, and I'd end up answering his fan mail and taking his phone messages. "Look, Chuck, you really don't want people to know you can talk. You'll never get any peace. Your life won't be any fun at all."

He raised a pudgy hand, stopping me from listing all the reasons why he should keep his mouth shut. "I'm way ahead of you, sis. I don't want fame. I just want to enjoy myself. I think I understand your viewpoint on all of this. We should be able to make a mutually agreeable deal."

"A deal?"

"Sure. You do whatever I ask, and I'll keep my mouth shut. Deal?"

I was about to say no, but I realized that it wasn't such a bad offer. How much could he ask? It was better than becoming the sister of the talking baby. "All right. You've got a deal."

It wasn't all that bad. It was more work than I expected, but I could handle it. Mostly, Chuck wanted me to read to him or make his favorite foods. On the positive side, Mom and Dad were thrilled to see how much time I was spending with my baby brother. I figured that it would put a crimp in my life for a year or two, but it would end when Chuck got old enough that his talking wasn't unusual. After that, I'd be finished.

I was just resting from a long session of swinging Chuck upside down. He loved that game, but it really tired me out.

So, I put him in his crib and dropped down on the couch. I hoped he'd take a nap. That's when I got most of my free time.

As I sprawled out on the couch, Mittens, my cat, came walking into the room. She hopped up on my lap, looked at me with those green eyes of hers, and said, "We have to talk."

"Huh?"

"You, me, and Sparks," Mittens said. She looked over toward the door. Sparks, my dog, trotted into the room, too.

"We don't want much," Sparks said. "I'm sure we can reach a mutually agreeable deal."

I sank farther down on the couch. My eyes fell on the goldfish. Her mouth was moving. "Not you, too," I said.

She nodded. A bubble slipped from her mouth. It rose to the surface and popped, spilling out the word, "Yup."

UNSEEN

I think I was eight or nine when I first started walking with my eyes closed. That was a couple years ago. In the beginning, I'd just take a step or two. I'd try to guess how far I was from something—like a stop sign or a fence. I'd walk up to a sign and reach out, trying to predict when my fingers would touch it. After a while, I got really good at it. Then I started going farther. I'd walk down the block, making my way from one corner to the next. I knew exactly where I was at every step. It was almost like my mind was seeing for me.

Even though I was pretty sure I knew what was in front of me, it took a long while before I could relax and really trust myself not to walk into something. Eventually, the fear vanished.

I started crossing the street. We live deep inside a development, and there isn't much traffic. Still, I kept my ears open, just in case there was a car or a bike or something.

I went farther and farther.

At first, I figured it would only work as long as I was

headed toward the last thing I saw. I'd stare ahead, burning everything into my memory. Then I'd close my eyes and walk. But one day, right in the middle of my straight path down the road, I turned a corner. I was able to keep going. I still knew where I was and what was ahead of me.

I started trying that about a month ago.

And a month ago, I started to notice something else. In the beginning, it was almost too small to catch my attention. I think the very first time I realized anything was happening, it was with a street sign. I'd seen the sign a thousand times: BELVIDERE BOULEVARD. When I opened my eyes to look at it, the letters had changed slightly. They were just a little wider.

At first, I thought it was my imagination. But I started to notice other changes. The color of a stop sign was a bit darker than I remembered. The initials carved in the bark of a tree seemed a bit deeper. All the changes were small.

The farther I went on any walk, the greater the changes became. If I went one block, nothing noticeable happened. But if I traveled a long way, the world definitely was different when I opened my eyes.

I started going even farther. I walked all the way around the block where I lived. My house had been made of red brick. When I opened my eyes, my house was covered with green siding.

I wondered if things would go back if I went the other way around the block. But that didn't happen. The siding didn't change.

Inside, I found that I didn't have a little sister anymore. I had a brother. I don't know whether that happened after my first or second trip around the block. But it was nice having a brother.

I decided to try walking all the way across town. When I reached the sign that read WELCOME TO FERNVALE, I opened my eyes. Then I turned and walked back home the normal way.

I still had a brother—that hadn't changed. Except he had seven toes on his left foot, which was kind of cool. And I guess I had rich parents. The house was bigger. There were all kinds of nice flowers in front, and huge trees filled with apples in back. It looked like a wonderful place to live.

I enjoyed my new life for a couple of days, but the urge to walk was too strong to resist. I set out this time for the big one—all the way to the edge of town and back to the house with my eyes closed. It was easy for me now—as easy as breathing. I couldn't wait to see the wonderful changes.

I went as far as the welcome sign. I reached out and touched it, feeling the spots where the paint was chipping, but I didn't open my eyes. I turned and started back. I got to my house with no trouble and reached out to touch the fence in front. As my hands brushed against the rusted metal, my eyes flew open. I hadn't meant to open them yet.

I wish I'd kept them closed.

The house was small and old and broken down. There was nothing in the yard but dead grass and weeds. I ran inside. Three kids—my three younger sisters—sat crying on the floor with their backs to me.

Had I gone too far? I needed to change things right away. I shut my eyes.

I *tried* to shut my eyes.

They wouldn't close.

I ran upstairs to the bathroom and looked in the mirror. Whatever I had become—whatever form of life I was, with a face like a rotting animal and a body like a gnome, I was a form of life that had no eyelids.

I covered my eyes with my hands, but it wasn't the same. I stumbled into the wall, then tripped and tumbled down the stairs to the living room.

Nearby, my sisters howled.

I dropped my hands and sat there, seeing everything. Unable to look away from the world I had created. Unable to create a different world.

FLYER*J*

The air grew cooler as a cloud drifted in front of the sun. Callie shivered in the sudden breeze that flowed around her, then looked down as a sheet of yellow paper sailed against her leg and stayed there, flapping like a snagged bird.

Litter, she thought, grabbing the sheet. *How disgusting.* There was something printed on the front in large letters: TOMORROW—10 PERCENT OFF EVERYTHING.

That's all that was there. Callie stared at the page for a moment, as if staring would reveal what was on sale or where the sale would be held. But no answer came.

Callie shrugged and released the flyer back into the wind that brought it. She didn't feel her action counted as littering, since someone else had obviously dropped the flyer in the first place.

She thought no more about it that day.

Something felt different the next morning. The world

was less bright. Callie's breakfast was less tasty. *Everything seems a little bit off*, she thought. Then her thoughts froze on an image of the flyer. "Ten percent off," she whispered.

The breeze brought another flyer that afternoon. TOMOR-ROW—ONE DAY ONLY—TWO-FOR-ONE SPECIAL. Callie spent half the night wondering what would come. In the morning, she rose to the delightful discovery that all the world was twice as nice as usual. Breakfast was doubly delicious. The weather was twice as beautiful as it had ever been. *One day only*, she thought, but what a fabulous and unforgettable day it turned out to be.

A week went by before the next flyer appeared. This one read—EXTENDED HOURS TOMORROW—OPEN EARLY, CLOSE LATE.

Sure enough, when Callie got up for school, the sun had already risen. When she went to bed, it was still light outside. As she fell asleep, she promised herself she'd find the source of the flyers.

In the morning, she stood in front of her house and tried to remember which way the wind had blown. Then she walked. She looked carefully in bushes and along the sides of buildings, following a trail of flyers. Finally, she found herself standing before a small house in the middle of an average street of small houses.

The garage door was open. Inside, she saw a machine. Callie realized it was a printing press. Another machine stood behind the press.

"Hello?" Callie called. She walked inside the garage. The

press was loaded with blank paper. The machine behind it had a series of buttons on one side. Above each button, Callie saw a sentence.

TOMORROW—10 PERCENT OFF EVERYTHING.

TOMORROW—ONE DAY ONLY—TWO-FOR-ONE SPECIAL.

The whole front of the machine was filled with phrases like these—row after row of buttons. Callie saw one that made her smile. SATISFACTION GUARANTEED. *How nice*, she thought. It would be great if that were true. She reached out and pressed the button beneath those words.

KACHANG!

Callie jumped away as the press sprang to life. It shot forward and back, spewing out the flyers.

Callie grabbed one of the sheets as it fluttered into the air. She smiled and started to read her creation. Her smile froze, then faded. On the flyer she saw no promise of satisfaction. No guarantee of happiness.

FIRE SALE, it read. EVERYTHING MUST GO.

"But . . . ?" Callie said. She looked at the machine. The line above the button had the words she wanted to print. The line below had the words she'd actually printed.

She'd pressed the wrong button. Callie curled her lip in disgust at the thought of a fire sale. She'd never been to one, but she knew that was where a store tried to get rid of merchandise that had been damaged in a fire.

Then Callie's gaze drifted out the door and up into the sky. FIRE SALE. Already, the sun seemed brighter. The air grew warmer. EVERYTHING MUST GO. In her hand, the flyer began to curl, its edges turning brown. Wisps of smoke drifted up from the flyer. The final flyer.

The sun grew even brighter. The air grew unbearably hot. Everything went.

EVERY AUTUMN

The best part about autumn was the piles of leaves. That's what Ted thought. He loved wading shin deep in the leaves, kicking his way through the crackling mounds that lined the curbs all around town. That was definitely the best part about autumn.

The worst part about autumn was *it*. That's what everyone called the thing that happened—*it*. "Do you think *it* will happen again?" they asked each other as autumn approached.

It always happened in the fall. Somewhere in the state, a kid vanished. Everyone in school talked about *it*. The amazing thing, to Ted, was that the adults didn't seem to believe there was a pattern—they didn't make the connection. But the kids all knew about *it*.

"Last year, it was a girl our age," Del said at lunchtime. "She lived way over in Mahony Township."

Kenny nodded. "That's what I heard. But the year before that, it was a boy just over in Switburg."

"No, he was from Sterling," Connor said.

"Somebody should do something," Ted said. "I looked in the paper. There's nothing."

"Yeah," Del said. "Adults don't believe there's any pattern."

Ted believed. So did his friends. Each afternoon, when he left school, he tried to make sure he was with other kids. But today, most of his friends had basketball practice. Ted was on his own.

As he walked home, he kept looking over his shoulder. That station wagon—hadn't it passed him once before? Ted tensed as the car cruised by. He looked around. There weren't any other kids in sight. The car seemed to slow as it went past Ted. Then it sped up again.

Ted was sure the driver had stared at him. He could feel the man's eyes studying him. Ted looked ahead. He was coming up to the corner by Hudson Street. Hudson was one way. That was good. He could turn there and the car couldn't follow. At least, not legally.

Ted hurried to the corner, then turned. He kept walking. There weren't any cars on Hudson Street.

Relax, he told himself as he stepped off the curb and into a pile of leaves. *Maybe it's all just talk.* He realized that the whole thing was silly. Now, far away from the wild rumors of his friends, he tried to think logically about *it*. Really, how could kids disappear without a trace every year? And why did *it* only happen in the fall? Why not summer or winter or spring?

As Ted swung his leg through the deep pile of leaves, his foot hit something. For an instant, he thought his foot was stuck. Then he felt a powerful grip tighten around his ankle. He realized he wasn't stuck—he was grabbed.

"Let go," Ted screamed, yanking his leg.

He couldn't get free. *It* had him.

It grabbed his other leg and pulled him beneath the leaves. As Ted disappeared from sight, he understood why *it* only happened in the fall.

A moment later, a station wagon came up Hudson Street the other way—the legal way. The driver, who was lost, scanned the sidewalks. He'd hoped to ask someone for directions. He'd seen a boy before, but he didn't want to scare him by stopping the car. He knew kids were taught to be careful about strangers. But even if he'd wanted to ask the boy, he couldn't now. There was nobody in sight. The streets were empty. It was almost as if the kid had vanished.

The driver headed down Hudson Street. Behind him, the piles of leaves swirled in the breeze of the passing car.

GOOSE EGGS

A goose is about the meanest and nastiest creature on the planet. That's how Charlie felt about those stupid, messy birds. He'd never seen anything that came close to being as unpleasant as a goose. And this goose, the one his little brother had named Honker, was no exception. If anything, it was even worse than most geese. From the moment it had wandered into their yard, Charlie hated it. He'd figured his folks would get rid of it, but Cliff had named it and claimed it.

His folks had gone along with the whole thing. After trying and failing to find out who owned the goose, they'd decided to keep it. "Well, Cliffy," his father had said, "it looks like you and Charlie have a new pet."

"Yippee," Cliff had shouted, jumping up and down and clapping his hands. "You hear that, Charlie? We get to keep Honker."

Charlie didn't say anything. Honker hissed. Then he tried to bite Charlie. Cliff laughed and squealed in delight.

And that's how Charlie found himself in the only family in town that had a goose for a pet.

Charlie never paid much attention to Honker, except to keep out of the goose's way. But one day, as he was walking through the backyard, he noticed something strange. Usually, Honker would chase him, biting at his legs as he walked past. But today, the goose was just sitting in the middle of the lawn.

Maybe it's sick, Charlie thought, unable to keep from smiling at the idea of the goose getting ill. "Your goose is cooked," he said out loud. Then he laughed.

Just as Charlie spoke, Honker stood for a moment, then settled back down. During that brief time, something glittered in the sunlight. *What was that?* Charlie wondered. He wandered closer to Honker, but the goose glared at him and hissed.

Charlie backed up. But he had to see what was under the goose. He waited for the bird to move. It stayed where it was.

"Whatcha doing?" Cliff asked when he wandered into the yard.

"Your goose is sitting on something," Charlie said. He really didn't want to tell Cliff, but maybe his brother would be able to get the goose to move.

Cliff walked over and reached beneath the goose. "Wow. An egg," he said, pulling out the object from under the bird.

Charlie just stared. It wasn't any ordinary egg—it was a golden egg. *Unbelievable.* He opened his mouth. Then he closed it.

"Look, Charlie, it's a golden egg," Cliff said. He didn't

seem to be surprised. Charlie had noticed that about little kids—they pretty much accepted anything that came along. They didn't know that, despite what they read in books or saw on TV, dogs didn't talk, fish didn't grant wishes, frogs didn't turn into princes, and geese certainly didn't lay golden eggs.

Charlie walked over and held his hand out. Cliff gave him the egg. "We have to hide this," Charlie said. He knew that he couldn't go around showing the egg to people. Gold made adults do funny things. He'd read stories—true stories—about people who'd done bad stuff to get gold. Charlie turned the egg slowly in his hand, then said, "We need to put it in a safe place."

"Where?" Cliff asked.

"My bottom drawer," Charlie said. The other drawers were for clothes. But the bottom drawer of the dresser was all Charlie's, and nobody else went there.

He hurried inside, carrying the egg upstairs to his room. "Don't tell anybody," he warned Cliff after he put it in his drawer.

"I won't," Cliff promised.

There was another golden egg beneath Honker the next day. And another the day after that.

"We can be kings," Cliff said as he held up the newest egg. "Or princes."

"I don't want to be a prince," Charlie said, taking the egg from his brother. He brought it upstairs and hid it with the others.

Honker kept laying golden eggs. Charlie kept putting

them in his drawer. After three weeks, his drawer was almost full.

That night, as Charlie was going to bed, Cliff said, "I've been thinking about it. You'd be a good prince."

"Whatever," Charlie said, trying to ignore his brother. He had other things on his mind. He had to do something with the eggs. Charlie thought about it as he went to brush his teeth. Maybe he should tell his parents. It was a wonderful secret, and he hated the thought of sharing it, but he didn't know what he was going to do with all the eggs.

Cliff was still in the room when Charlie got back. "Go to bed," Charlie told him. He watched his brother leave the room. Then he went to bed, too.

He closed his eyes and started to fall asleep. *I'll tell them about it tomorrow,* he thought as he drifted off.

His path toward sleep was disturbed by a clinking sound.

Charlie sat up, wondering what had made the strange noise.

There was another clink—like someone tapping a nickel with a spoon. Charlie stood and turned on his light.

The clink was coming from his drawer.

Charlie opened the drawer.

One of the eggs was moving—it shook with each clink. After a moment, a tiny crack appeared on the smooth, golden surface.

Why would a goose lay golden eggs? Charlie wondered. There had to be a reason.

What would people do with golden eggs?

Charlie realized they would do exactly what he had done—hide them out of sight in a drawer or a closet. They'd bring the eggs into their houses and keep them safe. It was a perfect place for something to wait until it was ready to hatch.

But what would be hatching from these eggs? A small piece of the egg fell away. Charlie looked inside. A bird was hatching. Charlie froze. He'd never seen a bird with a whole beakful of long teeth. He'd seen birds with claws, but never with claws like these.

The bird paused for a moment and looked at Charlie. Charlie looked back and remembered what he'd learned in school. Animals were usually hungry when they hatched. Lots of creatures laid their eggs where their young would have an easy time finding something to feed on.

What do people do with gold?

Charlie knew he had to get rid of all the eggs, and he had to do it quickly, before anything hatched. Once those creatures got free, they'd be dangerous. And hungry.

He grabbed a box from his closet and quickly filled it full of eggs. There didn't seem to be as many as he thought there'd be. Charlie checked the drawer again, making sure he hadn't missed any of the eggs. He knew it would be a disaster if he left even one.

They were all shaking now. Clinks filled the air, like someone was shaking a tray filled with silverware. It didn't seem to matter how long ago they'd been laid—they all looked like they were ready to hatch at once.

There was a storm drain outside by the curb. Charlie lugged the box down the steps and out the door. He reached the drain. The roar of water greeted him from below.

"So much for being rich," he said as he turned the box over and dumped the contents into the drain. As the eggs fell, the first hatching creature screamed at him, trying desperately to get free of the golden shell.

It didn't make it. The heavy eggs sank quickly in the rushing water. They tumbled far beneath the surface. The current carried the unhatched birds to their doom.

Charlie went back to bed.

He tried to sleep, but he couldn't. It had been too close. There was no telling what might have happened if he hadn't gotten rid of those eggs. When he closed his eyes, he could still see the head of that bird, with those awful teeth.

"Charlie," Cliff said, walking into the room.

"Go to sleep, Cliff," Charlie said.

"Maybe you can be a prince," Cliff said.

"Let it go," Charlie said. "Forget that nonsense."

"But you're awake," Cliff said. "That proves it."

"Proves what?" Charlie asked.

"Like with the princess in that story," Cliff said. "You know. They wanted to see if she was a real princess. They put a pea under her mattress. The pea kept her awake. I couldn't find a pea, so I used some eggs."

For a fraction of a second, Charlie didn't manage to put it all together. He had no idea what Cliff was talking about. During that instant, the birds ripped their way up through the mattress. During the next fraction of a second, as Charlie realized what Cliff had done, it became too late.

"Only a prince would feel anything," Cliff said.

Now Charlie felt them. He felt them all around as they burst through to the surface, scratching their way out from beneath the mattress, clawing and tearing their way to freedom. Newly hatched, they rushed into the world in search of their first meal.

FRESH FROM THE GARDEN

Mom, can I have a garden?" Judy stood in the backyard of the new house, looking at the wonderful space that stretched out in front of her.

"I don't see why not," her mom said. "As long as you do all the work. Deal?"

"Deal," Judy said. "Can I put it there?" she asked, pointing to a sunny spot next to a small bird feeder.

"Sure."

Judy got right to work. She dug up the grass, raked the soil, and removed all the stones. She'd learned about gardening from helping her neighbor in their old apartment in the city. Mr. Calderone had made a small garden at the back of the building between the parking lot and the fence. But this would be her very own garden.

The next day, Judy bought seeds for carrots, beans, and lettuce. She was glad they'd moved into the new house at just the right time for planting. Judy enjoyed working outdoors and spent most of each day in the backyard. Her room was nice, but it smelled a little strange. The odor reminded her of a hamster cage. Judy kept the windows open as much as possible, and eventually the smell went away.

Tending the garden helped keep Judy busy during those first weeks before she made any friends. Even after she'd met Ruth and Katie and the other girls in the neighborhood, Judy didn't talk about her garden. It was sort of a secret—something special she didn't want to share just yet. The other girls were nice enough, but Judy still felt like an outsider. She knew they'd accept her in time, as long as she didn't give them a reason to dislike her.

But the garden grew well—it grew beyond her wildest hopes, and the time came when she was ready to share.

"Can you come for lunch tomorrow?" she asked her new friends. "I've got a special treat for us."

"What is it?" Katie asked.

"You'll see." Judy smiled as she imagined Katie and Ruth enjoying a meal at her house.

"I can come," Ruth said.

"Me, too," Katie told her.

The next morning, Judy took her basket—a gift from her mother—and went out to the wonderful garden by the bird feeder. She pulled carrots from the soil and picked the most perfect beans and flawless lettuce she could find. By lunchtime, she'd made carrot sticks and a salad. Her mom had helped her cook the beans. Judy set the kitchen table, then put out small dishes of creamy dip for the carrots and bottles of three different dressings for the salad. Her friends arrived a few minutes later.

"Wow," Ruth said as she took her seat. "This looks great."

"Thanks." Judy felt that she had passed a test. She was one of them now.

"This is a lot nicer than when that creepy little Toby Mudmintz lived here," Ruth said.

"A boy lived here before me?" Judy asked.

Katie nodded. "Yeah. He was weird. Had all kinds of pets. He had tons of fish. And you know what?"

"What?" Judy asked.

Ruth's face scrunched up in disgust. "When the fish died, he didn't flush them. He always buried them out back. Can you imagine that? He had this whole section of the yard filled with fish and hamsters and birds. Snakes and lizards, too. Maybe even a couple guinea pigs. The kid was really weird. There were little tombstones all over the place. His mom made him take them down before they sold the house."

Judy paused, her fork just a tenth of an inch from impaling a piece of lettuce, and thought about the smooth, white stones she'd cleared from the garden. "Out back?"

"Yeah, out in the corner. I think there's a bird feeder or something there." Katie picked up a carrot stick. It seemed to wriggle slightly in her hand.

Judy looked at the lettuce. The edges rippled, fluttering like the fins of a tropical fish.

Crunch . . .

She looked up as Katie chomped on the carrot stick. "Wow—this is really juicy," Katie said after she'd finished chewing. "And very fresh."

"Yum, fabulous string beans," Ruth said. She lifted a forkful. The ends waved slightly. "It's so nice of you to share this with us. I'm glad you moved here. We're going to be such good friends. Could you pass the carrots?"

Judy slid the plate toward Ruth, happy to move it farther away from herself.

"Aren't you going to eat?" Katie asked. "There's nothing wrong, is there?" She glanced down at her plate, and a frown crossed her lips.

"No," Judy said, quickly. "Nothing's wrong. Nothing at all." She plunged the lettuce into a puddle of dressing, covering the leaf completely, then lifted the fork to her mouth.

Judy took a deep breath, then swallowed the lettuce whole. It seemed to wriggle as it went down her throat. She shuddered, but managed not to gag. She was pretty sure that with the help of lots of dressing, she could get through this one lunch. Then it would all be over. She clenched her jaw as a wave of nausea shot through her stomach. *You can make it,* she told herself. It would be worth it to have friends.

"Let's do this again," Ruth said. She dabbed at the corner of her lip with her napkin.

"Let's do this lots," Katie said as she stabbed a forkful of beans. They let out a squeaky little scream when the tines pierced their bodies. "I could eat fresh vegetables like this every day. They're wonderful. So young and tender. Can we come back tomorrow?"

"Yeah," Ruth said, snapping a carrot stick in half. A spray of juice splattered across the table. "Is tomorrow okay?"

Judy nodded, not trusting herself to open her mouth.

THE COVERED BRIDGE

There was only one way to get to town. Only one road that crossed the river. The river wasn't bad, even though the water got a bit high and rough when the heavy rains came in early spring or late fall. The road wasn't bad, even though it grew narrow in parts and twisted back and forth through the hills, sometimes in such a blind curve that Carol was sure her mom or dad would smash into an oncoming car before they got through the turn.

But there was rarely anything on the road in the other direction, and they never met another car on the tight curves. No, Carol didn't mind the road that much. But there was something about the bridge—the old wooden covered bridge that swallowed up the car and bathed it with shadows. There was something Carol hated.

"That bridge gives me the creeps," she said to her friend Jackie one evening as they sat on Carol's porch.

"That's not creepy," Jackie said.

"It is to me," Carol said.

Jackie shook her head. "I'll tell you what's creepy. Marigots. Those are creepy." She shuddered.

"What's that?"

"My grandma told me about them. She said they come out once every fifty years, if the conditions are right. They only come out for an hour. They're like fat earthworms. But they eat meat. They have teeth. She said they're about due to come back."

"That's crazy," Carol said, feeling a slight shiver run down her shoulders and along her arms. She didn't want to hear any more about such nonsense. Even made-up stuff could be spooky after the sun went down.

"It's true." Jackie jumped up and pointed toward the yard. Her eyes opened wide. Her mouth moved for a moment, but no sound came out. Finally, the scream broke free. "THERE'S ONE!"

Carol leaped from her seat and pressed her back against the wall next to the front door. "Where?"

"Got you." Jackie started laughing.

"Jackie! That's not nice." Carol tried to relax, but she could feel her heart slamming against her ribs.

"Sorry," Jackie said. "I couldn't resist. You should have seen your face. Come on. I've got to go. Walk me partway."

"Just as far as the bridge," Carol said.

"Not across?"

"Nope." She'd tried to keep her fear hidden so nobody

would make fun of her, but she had a feeling her friend might have guessed her secret.

Jackie shrugged and got up. Carol followed her down the road to the bridge.

Twice, Jackie stopped and shouted, "THERE'S ONE!"

Both times, Carol jumped. Both times, Jackie giggled.

"Well," Jackie asked when they reached the bridge. "You going to walk me any farther?"

Carol shook her head. If she went over the bridge with Jackie, that meant she'd have to go back across by herself.

Jackie sprinted ahead to the middle of the bridge. She was nearly lost in the shadows. All Carol could see was a vague form.

"Come on. Just walk a few steps with me. I wouldn't make you go across by yourself."

Carol took a deep breath. If she walked just a little way with Jackie, she'd be able to keep her in sight when she went back to her own side. "Stay right there," she said, hating how timid she sounded.

She stepped onto the bridge. The wood, built to take the weight of cars and trucks, didn't creak beneath her feet. "Jackie? You there?" The form didn't seem to be getting any closer. Carol walked, bracing herself, expecting Jackie to jump at her and shout *Boo!* any moment.

"Jackie?" she called again.

There was no answer. Carol froze, unsure whether to go ahead and search for Jackie or to run back. She took another step, and another. Finally, ahead, she saw dim light.

The night, dark but brighter than the inside of the bridge, revealed Jackie standing to the side of the road about ten feet away.

Carol ran forward, pausing at the very edge of the bridge. She was too angry with Jackie to join her on the ground. "You didn't wait for me."

"Hey. I did you a favor. You made it. Now you know there's nothing to be scared of. So you can stop being such a baby about the bridge."

Before Carol could answer, something caught her eye. All around Jackie, small mounds pushed up in the soil. At first, Carol thought it was a trick of the shadows. She realized it was no trick when she saw hundreds of slimy, wriggling creatures bursting from the holes. Even in the dark, their teeth gleamed bright.

"Jackie! Look out!" Carol screamed, reaching out toward her friend. "Hurry!"

"Yeah. Ha, ha. You got me," Jackie said, taking a step away from the bridge. "Oh boy, am I scared. Nice try."

Those were the last words she ever spoke. Carol stared in horror as the marigots swarmed over Jackie, dragging her down. She froze, terrified, unable to turn away from the sight, unable to run.

It wasn't until well after the marigots slithered back into the ground that Carol's brain began to function again. *I'm alive*, she realized. That was her first thought. Her second thought brought a strange smile to her lips. There was a reason why she had survived. The marigots had something in common with her. They, too, must have been afraid of the bridge.

Carol turned. She still had to cross the bridge to get back home. That was okay. Somehow, it just didn't seem all that scary anymore.

BUZZ OFF

I could never have sat still the way Adam Selkirk did when the bee landed on his hand. Maybe he didn't notice it right away. But I sure did.

"Adam, there's a bee on your hand," I said, moving away from him. We were hanging out at the school playground after dinner—me, Adam, Blinky Foster, and Michael Altman. We'd been wrestling and had just plopped down on the ground to cool off.

Adam looked at his hand. "Dad says they can smell fear."

"That's dogs or wolves or something," Michael told him. "Bees can't smell."

"Then how do they find flowers?" I asked as I watched the bee crawl along Adam's knuckles like a hiker going over hills.

"Ultraviolet light," Blinky said. "Don't any of you guys read *Scientific American?*"

"Yeah, every day," I said. I reached out and smacked Blinky on the head. Not hard. Just playing.

"Careful," Adam said through clenched teeth. "Don't make any sudden moves."

"That's you who shouldn't make sudden moves," Michael told him. He swung his hands through the air, then did a couple jumping jacks and an awkward flying kick. "See, I can move as much as I want. So, how about I all of a sudden hit the bee?"

"No," Adam said. "Then I'll get stung for sure."

I watched the bee walk to the tip of Adam's index finger. It stood there, looking like it was about to take off. Instead, another bee flew over and landed next to it, right behind the nail on Adam's middle finger.

"Oh no," Adam groaned.

"Shoulda let me smack it," Michael said.

"Just wave your hand," I told Adam. "They'll fly off."

"No. I'll get stung," Adam said.

The two bees seemed to be exchanging greetings. It was actually kind of fun to watch them, especially since I didn't figure I was in any danger.

It got even more interesting when the third bee landed on the back of Adam's hand.

"Wow, consider the odds against that happening," Blinky said. "Then again, each additional bee makes the next one more likely, wouldn't you say?" He looked around at us like he expected some kind of response.

Michael responded by hitting Blinky on the head.

The next two bees landed together on Adam's arm.

"See," Blinky said. "This definitely reduces the odds against it happening again."

Michael slapped him again. Then he looked at Adam and said, "Want me to go get some bug spray from home?"

"I don't know," Adam said.

I suspect he was weighing the risks of getting stung against the risks of getting sprayed by some chemical that might make him really sick. We all knew how that stuff was covered with warning labels.

"You know what I heard?" Michael asked. "I heard that Peter Forbushe's little brother got into some bug spray and now they have to take out his kidneys."

As the rest of us considered that news in silence, three more bees came in for a landing on Adam's shirt. I moved another foot or two away from him.

Adam shifted like he was going to try to get up. The bees all buzzed a bit louder. Adam sighed and settled down. "They have to leave sooner or later," he said.

"Yeah," I agreed. "They have to."

"Not necessarily," Blinky said. "When you consider—" He stopped as he noticed Michael getting ready to slap him on the head again.

So far, none of the bees had left Adam. Three bees landed on his leg. Seconds later, two more landed on his hand. "I think you're past the swatting stage," I said. With one bee, he'd had a chance. Now, there was no chance he could swat his way out of trouble.

I noticed Adam had gotten a bit farther away from me. He couldn't move, so I guess I must have snuck a few more feet from danger. Who could blame me?

"What kind of spray you got?" Adam asked.

Michael shrugged. "Just stuff. You know. Dad has it in the garage. Want me to get it?"

Before Adam could answer, a bee landed on his lip.

I'd been thinking about leaving, but now I had to stay and see what happened. The bee crawled across Adam's lip, then started investigating his nose.

"Maybe it's looking for a place to build a new hive," Blinky said.

"Huh?" Adam asked. I could tell he was trying really hard not to move his lips.

"Just kidding," Blinky said.

Something flew past my face and I swatted at it without thinking. But it was only a mosquito. It was starting to get dark and the bugs were coming out.

That's when Michael looked at me and jumped away.

"What?" I asked. "What is it?"

He just pointed at my back.

Blinky looked, then he moved away, too.

"Bees?" I asked.

Michael shook his head.

I tried to look at my back. As I turned, there was a loud buzzing. All the bees on Adam flew off as if something had scared them. But I didn't care about that. I cared about the glimpse I got of my back.

"How many?" I asked.

"Three," Blinky said. "No, wait, make that four." He moved several more paces away from me.

Another one landed on my shoulder. I wanted to run, but I didn't want to startle it. I had no idea whether it might bite me. I really didn't know anything about bats.

Something landed on my head.

Michael took off. I looked at Adam and Blinky. "Stay with me," I pleaded.

"Sorry," Adam said. He ran after Michael.

"And you?" I asked Blinky.

He took a step away from me, and then another step. "Look on the bright side," he said.

"Ut?" I asked, unable to move my lips enough to say *what* without startling the bat that was resting on my left cheek.

"They're mammals," Blinky said. "At least they'll keep you from getting too cold."

I guess he left right after that, but I can't say for sure. When the next bat landed, I closed my eyes. Then I tried to get comfortable. It looked like it was going to be a long night—a warm one, but a long one.

JUST DESSERTS

The nice thing about being a kid, as far as Dylan was concerned, was that he could sleep while the adults did the boring stuff like driving. So, even though it was tough waking up at four in the morning, he knew he could go back to sleep as soon as he got into his Uncle Harold's car.

But it didn't work that way. Uncle Harold, Cousin Roy, and Uncle Harold's friends talked and laughed and carried on for the whole two-hour drive. All the way from home to the ocean, Dylan barely managed to get any sleep. He tried, but it was no use. When he finally managed to drift off, he felt Uncle Harold shaking him.

"Rise and shine, sleepyhead."

"I'm up," Dylan said, looking out the car window. They were parked next to a boat dock. A sign read: CHARTER TRIPS. BLUEFISH, WRECK FISHING, ALL-DAY OR HALF-DAY CHARTERS.

"That our boat?" he asked.

"Yuppers," Uncle Harold said.

Dylan followed the others to the trunk of the car, where they unloaded their stuff. Dylan had brought a lunch his mom had made. It was in Uncle Harold's cooler, along with a lot of other food. As far as Dylan could tell from the conversations he heard all around him, the men were almost as excited about eating as they were about fishing.

They boarded the boat, where they met the rest of the group. There were about fifteen people, altogether. Everyone seemed to know everyone else. This was Dylan's first time out, but his uncle and cousin had been going on deep-sea trips for years.

"You're gonna have a ball," Uncle Harold said, slapping Dylan on the back.

"Great." Dylan took a seat on a bench along one side of the boat. Roy plopped down next to him. The sky was brighter now. The sun washed the water with streaks of red. The boat cruised out of the dock area, then picked up speed.

"Will we be there soon?" Dylan asked.

"Yeah, just an hour or two."

For an instant, Dylan figured he'd heard wrong. "Did you say an hour or two?"

"Sure thing," Roy said. "Have to get out to the good spots."

"We can't just stop here and fish?" Dylan asked. He looked around. It was all just ocean. What did it matter where they went?

"Nope, have to find the fish," Roy said. He nodded toward the cabin that was behind them. "Get something to eat from the cooler," he suggested.

"I'm saving it for later," Dylan said. He didn't want to eat his lunch yet. It wasn't even time for breakfast. He got up and wandered around the boat. It was kind of fun shooting across the water and bumping over the waves, but Dylan was pretty sure it would get boring after a couple of hours. He thought about taking a nap, but he doubted he could sleep on the boat while it was doing so much bouncing.

Dylan walked all the way around the boat. There were benches on each side. And there were tubes where people could put their rods. He saw a guy at the back of the boat preparing the bait. Dylan watched him for a while and asked him a few questions, but the guy didn't seem to want to talk.

Dylan walked over to his uncle, but the men were smoking these really stinky cigars, so Dylan went back to his seat next to Roy. "Great," Dylan muttered when he realized that Roy was asleep. He sat and waited. Eventually, the roar of the engine dropped to a hum and the boat slowed down. All around him, there were finally signs of action. The first mate handed out fishing rods and buckets of bait. Roy actually woke up.

"Time to fish?" Dylan asked.

"Soon," Roy said.

"Soon? Aren't we stopping?"

"Have to anchor, first," Roy said. "Takes a few minutes."

"Oh." Dylan waited. A half hour later, the boat was finally anchored and everyone started fishing.

Dylan figured he'd be enjoying himself now, except that the fish weren't biting. He could hear people talking about how great it had been the last trip.

"So many fish, my arms got tired," Roy told him.

An old guy sat down on the other side of Dylan. He chattered at Dylan for a while, complaining about feeling seasick, but then he fell asleep. Dylan wondered why people went to all the trouble to take the trip way out here, and then just slept.

After several hours, Dylan figured he'd waited long enough. He was bored, and the only thing he could think to do was eat his lunch. At least that would kill some time.

Dylan went into the cabin. He opened the cooler, took out the brown paper bag, and brought it back to his spot on the bench. "Well, something good finally happened," he said when he saw that his mother had packed one of those fruit pies he really liked. It was a cherry pie—the kind with the sugar glaze on top and the extremely sweet filling.

For a moment, Dylan was tempted to eat the pie first, but he decided to save it for last. So he ate his salami sandwich and his pretzels and drank a soda. Then he held the pie in his hands, looking at the unopened wrapper. *In a bit*, he thought.

The long day was finally catching up with him. The food and the rocking of the boat were making him sleepy. He noticed that the old guy was still asleep. Roy, on his right, was awake, but he hadn't caught anything.

Dylan fell asleep.

He dreamed that he'd caught a shark. It fought for hours, but he brought it in. When he pulled it out of the water, it had Uncle Harold's face.

Dylan woke up.

It took him a minute to realize that something was wrong. Roy was gone. The old guy was gone. *They're playing a joke on me*, he thought. He stood, trying to stay calm.

"Uncle Harold," he called, inching along one side of the boat.

There was nobody in sight.

Feeling foolish for doing it, Dylan walked to the rail and looked over the side of the boat. There was nothing to see in the water. Some of the rods were in their holders. Others were on the deck. It looked like they'd been dropped.

"Come on, this isn't funny," Dylan called. He walked all the way around the boat.

He was alone.

There was no place where everyone could hide. Dylan looked at the bench. His paper bag was still there, smoothed out and flattened down the way he'd left it, with the un-opened pie sitting on top of it. His mouth watered. *In a minute*, he thought. In a minute, he'd sit and eat his pie, and think things out.

There had to be something he could do. The radio. That was it. Dylan turned to walk across the deck to the cabin door.

That's when it grabbed him.

For the first few horrible seconds, all Dylan knew was that something had taken hold of him. It was wet and slimy. He pulled at it and yanked at the tentacle, but he didn't have a chance. It was far stronger than he was.

Dylan struggled as the creature dragged him closer to the railing. It was no use. As he was pulled over the side, he got one final glimpse of the bench. Dylan's eyes locked on his pie—the pie he'd been saving for last.

I should have eaten it first, he thought as he was dragged into the ocean.

THE WHOLE NINE YARDS

Most people around here don't know much about concrete. Actually, most of the people around here call concrete "cement." And that's just plain wrong. I should know. I used to live near a cement factory. The entire town was covered with white dust. Dad could never get the car clean. Mom was always washing the front of the house with the hose. But lots of folks had jobs at the factory, so we put up with the pollution.

Until we moved, that is. Then we got fresh air. It's pretty nice out here in Arizona. I've made a couple of friends already. I was walking with one of them, Scott Barnes, when we saw a new patch of sidewalk.

"Cool," Scott said, rushing up to the wooden sawhorse that blocked off the concrete. "Look at that cement. And it's not even dry."

"Concrete," I said.

"Whatever." He pointed to the middle. "Check that out."

I looked. Then I laughed. Someone had managed to

leave a pair of footprints right in the middle of the concrete. I didn't have a clue how they'd done it. There were no other footprints, and no sign of a splash or anything. The strangest thing was that there wasn't any tread—the print was flat and smooth. Maybe whoever had done it was wearing old sneakers.

Scott kneeled down and touched the surface of the slab. "Darn, it's dried already. I wanted to write my initials."

"Cured." I told him. "Concrete doesn't dry—it cures. How do you think they use it underwater for bridges?"

"You need to be cured," Scott said. He looked back at the sidewalk. "One of these days, I'm going to get to the cement in time and leave my mark—you know, my initials. Just once—that's all I ask. Just one *SB* written to last forever."

I shrugged. I guess everyone had different dreams. We headed down the street. A while later, we saw another sawhorse. Scott picked up the pace and jogged over. Once again, he knelt down and checked out the concrete.

"Dry," he said, getting back up.

"Cured," I said.

"Hey," he said, ignoring my comment, "maybe they're doing a bunch of sidewalks today."

"Could be. One truck holds a lot. As a matter of fact, a whole load is nine cubic yards," I told him. "That's where the expression comes from."

"What expression?" Scott asked.

"The whole nine yards."

"You're crazy—that comes from football," he said.

I didn't bother arguing. Scott hurried down the street. He seemed to be on a mission. "Gonna leave my mark," he said.

As I walked after him, I looked back. There was a set of footprints in this patch of concrete, too. I had no idea how the kid had done it. I really thought I knew everything about concrete and cement. As I turned away from the spot, I realized that I had a bit of a mission myself. While Scott was running around, trying to find a place to leave his mark, I was going to go with him, hoping to get a chance to see how that kid was leaving those footprints.

We wandered up and down the side streets. We found two more slabs of recently poured sidewalk, but they'd already cured. Each spot seemed a bit fresher than the previous one. I figured we were getting close.

"That's it," Scott said, looking ahead as we caught sight of another sawhorse. "I know this is the one."

He ran ahead. I saw him kneel down. Then he almost jumped for joy as he shouted, "Yes!"

I caught up with him. There was a small mark where he'd tested the concrete with his finger. Otherwise, the surface was perfectly smooth. There wasn't even a footprint. "Finger or a stick?" Scott asked.

"What?"

"Come on—you're the big expert. What works better? Should I use my finger? Or should I look for a stick?"

I shrugged. "Either way would work. Some people are allergic to concrete, but it's not that common."

"Great. Here we go. Ess," he said as he drew his first initial into the concrete. He lifted his finger and paused for a second, then grinned. "Finally, I'm doing something that will last." He reached down and added the B.

"Oops, one more thing, just to make it perfect." He raised his finger and thrust it down, making a period after the S. Then he made a period after the B.

"Okay, you've left your mark. Now let's get out of here," I said.

"I can't," Scott said.

"What?"

"My finger's caught."

"Quit joking." I looked over his shoulder. He still had his finger stuck in the concrete. He was pulling, but it wouldn't come out. I figured he was fooling around, trying to play a trick on me.

I changed my mind when he was yanked in up to his elbow with one sudden jerk. "Get help," he said.

"Yeah." But before I could take a step, he got dragged down and across the concrete. His body slid over the spot where he'd written his initials, smoothing the surface out. A moment later, he got pulled under. It wasn't like someone sinking in quicksand. It was fast. One second, he was only sunk in up to his arm. The next, he got tugged down. For an instant, there was nothing to see but his ankles and feet. The laces of his sneakers dangled, lying on the surface of the concrete.

Then he got pulled completely under. I heard a plop. As his feet sunk down, there must have been some kind of suction. They left behind two marks like footprints.

116

As I watched, the rest of the surface smoothed itself over. But the footprints stayed there. Right below them, the concrete bulged for a second. Then a bubble burst through, making a sound a lot like a burp. I waited a minute, to see if there would be anything more, but nothing else disturbed the surface. The concrete was already beginning to cure, leaving those two perfect footprints.

So that's how it happened. And I thought I knew everything about concrete.

THE GREEN MAN

We all spent a good part of the spring creeped out by the Green Man. I don't know when the stories started, or where I first heard them, but everyone was talking about him by late May.

"He's not human," Ethan said. "He's some kind of lizard or something."

"You don't know what you're talking about," Danny told Ethan. "He's human. But he's got wings or something."

"He used to be a cop, that's what I heard."

"No, he was in the army. Something went wrong with an experiment."

"He's not from this planet."

That's how it went. Every day on the playground, there were new reports of sightings. The Green Man wasn't actually ever seen by the person telling the story. It was always someone else. Mary heard he'd been spotted on the roof of the school by one of the teachers. She wasn't sure which one.

Eldridge said that the janitor had chased the Green Man

out of the storage room. Or maybe it wasn't our school—maybe it had happened across town at the high school.

My best friend, Rob, swore his older brother knew someone who had seen the Green Man in the woods behind the town pool.

I noticed that the Green Man wasn't ever seen alone. He had an animal with him. Most kids said it was a collie. This was the only part of the story that wasn't creepy. I'd never known a mean collie. They were great dogs. If the Green Man was real, I doubted he had a collie. I found it easier to believe the versions that mentioned something wild like an eagle or a wolf. I didn't pay much attention to the really weird stuff, like Danny's claim that the Green Man ran around with a jackal.

Even if some of the stories were hard to swallow, I couldn't help believing in the Green Man. And because I believed, I couldn't help feeling twitches of fear in my gut. Nobody knew what he was capable of doing. He was a shadowy figure. But there was always a hint of danger in the sightings.

When I walked anywhere alone, I checked over my shoulder constantly. I'd scan the rooftops and tense up as I approached each potential hiding place—a large tree, a parked car, anything that might conceal the Green Man. At night, every small sound sent me to the window. A branch scraping against the house was enough to wake me. I slept with the Green Man slithering through my mind.

I'd always tried to face the things that scared me. When I was little, I used to be afraid of the basement. One day, I made myself climb halfway down the steps in the dark. I'd wanted to go all the way down, but halfway was as far as I could push myself. Still, I went and I sat on the steps, and nothing grabbed me and dragged me down or fell on me and drained my blood. I don't think I'm brave—I'm just stubborn. It annoys me when something scares me. So I deal with it.

"I'm going to find him," I told Rob as we sat behind the school watching the younger kids playing kickball.

"Who?"

"The Green Man."

"Yeah, right." Rob shook his head. "Get me his autograph, okay? And get one from the dog, too. I'm sure he can write."

"I'm serious. If there's a real Green Man, I'm going to find him. I'm tired of hearing all these stories. Don't you want to know if he's real?"

"No way. I don't want anything to do with him."

I listened to every story, no matter how weird, and marked each sighting on a map I'd taped to my bedroom wall.

There was a pattern.

The sightings swirled around a single center—the town pool. That's where he was. If he was real, he lived near the pool. If he wasn't real, why would there be a pattern?

"I think I found him," I told Rob. "I'm going to check it out this weekend."

"Maybe you should just tell some adults," Rob said. "Let them take care of it."

"They wouldn't listen to me."

There was no way Rob could argue about that. We both knew that grown-ups didn't really pay attention to kids, and they certainly didn't listen to them when the subject was something like the Green Man.

I had no idea how to search for him. I didn't know whether to sneak around or to shout for his attention. I went to the pool—it was still drained and empty, awaiting the return of summer—and stood by the fence.

If I were the Green Man, where would I go when I wasn't haunting rooftops?

There were woods behind the pool. He might live in a tent or something. Maybe he didn't need man-made shelter. Maybe he just tunneled into the ground like a giant worm or glided across the tree branches like a python.

I strolled along the fence. At one end, there was a shed that held supplies for the pool. The door wasn't quite closed.

I walked over to the shed and put my hand against the edge of the door. In my mind, I saw a scene unfold. It was a daydream, I guess. Maybe it was my way of dealing with the fear. I imagined that I looked through the opening and saw a figure sitting on a box near a corner of the shed.

Are you the Green Man? I asked him.

No, he said. *Please come in.*

I stepped inside. He stayed in the shadows. I moved closer. He raised his head and spoke. *Actually,* he said, extending his hand toward me, holding it right up in front of my eyes, *I think this is closer to blue.*

Then I saw his face, and it was the face of a lizard. In the corner, a collie growled. Man and dog dove at me.

I shuddered, trying to fling the image from my mind. My hand squeezed the door of the shed. I held my breath and listened.

The raspy sound of another breath leaked from inside. The Green Man was there. I knew it.

He must have known I was outside.

Face my fears or run? I opened the door an inch. I opened it another inch. A new scene raced through my mind. As I stepped inside, he spread his wings and flew at me, all fangs and claws. His dog had wings, too.

I wrestled with my thoughts for a moment, then opened the door farther. Not knowing what else to do, I called, "Hello?" The word sounded stupid as it fell from my lips. I cleared my throat and called out again.

There was no reply, but a rustling sound drifted from the far left corner of the cluttered shed. The single window in the back wall was too dirty to let in much light. I stepped into the doorway. He was huddled against the wall, wrapped in a blanket. He hadn't shaved in a long time. He wasn't much older than my father, but he was thin and tired. No threat to me.

"Sorry," I said. That didn't seem to be enough. I had to fill the empty space between us with words of explanation. "I was looking for the Green Man."

I turned to leave. As I stepped away, his words caught me. "The Green Man." He let out a sound somewhere between a laugh and a cough. "I remember him. We used to be so scared—back when we were kids."

I looked over my shoulder. "You know about the Green Man?"

He nodded. "Just a story. Just something kids scare each other with. Wait until you grow up. Then you'll find real things to be scared of." He started coughing again.

"Can I do anything for you?"

He shook his head.

"Are you sure?" I asked

"I'm sure."

As I walked away, I wondered if I should tell someone about him. Maybe there were people who could help him. A few paces later, I realized I'd left the door open. The cool air would blow into the shed. I turned back to close the door. Right then, I heard a whistle from inside. It was a short, loud whistle—just one note.

Something shot past my legs, so close I almost tumbled over it. A furry shape, running on four paws, dove through the doorway into the shed.

For a heartbeat, I froze, trying to catch my balance. Then I flung open the door. I got there just in time to see them leaving by the window. The dog—if that's what it was—had already escaped out the back. The man—if that's what he was—still straddled the sill. The blanket lay discarded on the floor. Green tattoos covered his arms. Even his face, in the light of the window, had a greenish cast to it.

Somehow, I spoke. "You're him, aren't you?"

He looked back at me. "It doesn't really matter who I am," he said, his voice no longer feeble and tired. "You make your own fears. That's how it works." He slipped outside and ran off, following the beast.

I watched the Green Man fade into the woods. I had a funny feeling he'd go somewhere else now. Or maybe there were many Green Men. Maybe each town had one. I really didn't understand what had happened—at least, not all of it. But I figured he was there to give us a fear we could deal with, since so much of what we faced each day was out of our control. Or maybe he was there because our fears had made him real.

But as I watched him vanish into the distance, I realized that I was no longer afraid of the Green Man. In a way, that knowledge made me sad. I'd lost something. In a way, it also worried me. I wondered what would show up to take his place.

DIZZY SPELLS

Faster!" Monty screamed. He leaned out as far as he could, gripping the metal pipe with one hand, squeezing so hard that his fingers grew numb. He thrust his other hand out and let the wind smash against his face and rip at his hair. "Faster!"

Carl grunted as he managed one last burst of speed. Monty felt the merry-go-round respond to the push. Then it slowed as Carl stopped pushing and jumped aboard.

Monty closed his eyes and let the motion carry him.

"Oh boy," Monty said as he stepped off the ride once it had slowed to a stop. He staggered a bit. The world was still spinning inside his head. "That was great. Want to go again?"

"I've had enough," Carl said. "If I get any dizzier, I think I'll puke."

"I wish you hadn't said that," Monty told him. His stomach had felt fine until then.

"Said what?" Carl asked.

"You know—you said you'd puke."

"No, I didn't," Carl said.

"Yes, you did," Monty insisted. "You just said it right now."

"Did not."

Monty sighed. There was no point in arguing. He forgot about it quickly enough. Until the next week, when the thing with the baseball bat happened.

They'd seen it on television. Put a bat on the ground with the handle sticking up. Put your forehead on the bat and run around in a circle five times. Then pick up the bat and try to hit a ball.

Monty watched as Carl went first. Carl turned in a tight circle. Then he straightened up and tossed the ball. He almost fell over when he swung at it. He tried again and missed. By then, he was laughing so hard he didn't have any chance of hitting it.

"My turn," Monty said, grabbing the bat. He leaned over and put his forehead against the handle, then started going in a circle.

When he stood up, the whole world was spinning. Monty could barely stay on his feet. He'd never been so dizzy before. He tossed the ball, swung, and missed. He leaned over and tried to pick up the ball, but he fell to his knees. Finally, he managed to get back up. "I wish I could hit it right over the fence," he said.

Monty tossed the ball. He swung hard and whacked it right over the fence.

"Holy cow," Carl said.

"Wow . . ." Monty, still dizzy, watched the ball drop over the fence at the edge of the playground.

That's when he knew.

All he had to do was get dizzy, and his wishes would come true.

"I wish I had a million dollars," he said.

Nothing happened.

Monty realized he wasn't very dizzy. He put the bat down and started spinning again.

"Hey," Carl said. "It's my turn."

Monty ignored Carl and kept spinning around the bat. Finally, he stopped and said, "I wish I had every video game in the world."

His wish didn't come true.

"What's going on?" Carl asked.

Monty explained. When he was finished, he realized what the problem was. "I bet I have to get dizzier each time. Otherwise it doesn't work."

"Hey, let's spin you on the swings. That'll do it."

"Great idea," Monty said. He ran to the swings and sat down. Carl grabbed the chains on either side of the swing and started twisting them around, winding Monty tighter and tighter.

"Ready?" he asked when the chains were as tight as they could be.

"Ready," Monty said.

Carl let go. Monty started to unwind. The swing went faster and faster until Monty felt that the whole world was a blur. When it unwound and started to wrap the other way,

Monty jumped off. He was so dizzy, he could barely think. He was sure he was dizzier than before. He wondered whether he had to make the wish before the dizziness wore off.

"I wish I had a horse," he said.

"Are you crazy?" Carl asked. "What did you wish that for?"

"I couldn't think of anything else," Monty said. "I was—"

He stopped at the sound of a whinny. Right behind Carl, there stood a very big horse. "Oh, great. What am I going to do with a horse," Monty said. He took a step toward the horse. It let out another whinny and ran off.

"What a waste," Carl said. "You could have gotten something good. Come on. Let's try it again."

"Okay." Monty sat on the swing, but he had his doubts. They tried and tried until Monty couldn't stand it anymore. But none of the wishes came true.

"I need to get dizzier," he said. He looked at Carl and Carl looked back. Monty knew the answer. He could tell that Carl did, too.

"The Spinulator!" Carl said, naming the most awesome, brain-scrambling, twisting, turning, spinning ride on the planet.

"Let's go." Monty went home and broke into his savings bank. It didn't matter how much he spent. When he got off the Spinulator, he was going to wish for a million dollars.

They caught the bus to the next town, then walked to the entrance to Action World. The two admissions took almost all Monty's money. He didn't mind.

"Here goes," he said when he and Carl were strapped into the ride.

It was wild. Half the time, Monty couldn't even tell whether he was right side up or upside down. He was whipped and spun and twisted and tossed like pizza dough.

Finally, the ride stopped. Monty staggered off, so dizzy he thought his eyes would bounce out of his head.

What was it he was going to ask for? He tried to think. His brain was sloshing inside his head like a bowl of soup. If only he could think clearly for a moment. "I wish the world would stop spinning," he said.

"No!" Carl shouted as the wish escaped from Monty's lips. "Take it back."

Too late. The world stopped spinning.

Unfortunately, everything on it kept moving.

As Monty hurtled through the air, he remembered another wish he'd had when he was little. He'd wished he could fly.

Screaming and tumbling, but not tumbling enough to become very dizzy, Monty finally got that wish, too.

THE TANK

Jeremy didn't make it a habit to stare into toilets. But he couldn't help noticing when the calm surface of the water in the bowl suddenly rippled. He was in the bathroom brushing his teeth, and his eyes just happened to settle on the toilet at the right moment. He watched the water grow calm. A moment later, another ripple spread from the center of the bowl.

Strange, Jeremy thought as he turned away from the toilet and finished brushing his teeth. He looked back at the water when he was done, but it remained flat and motionless.

That night, as he was lying in bed, Jeremy heard a hollow boom, like someone had hit a gigantic empty oil drum with the side of a clenched fist. The boom seemed far off, and only happened once. *Could be anything*, Jeremy thought. *It's not important.*

He fell asleep soon after, and slept well. In the morning, when he went to the bathroom, he noticed that the water in the toilet was rocking and settling down, as if it had just splashed up a moment earlier.

That night, when he got in the tub, he could feel something pulsing through the water, beating against the drainpipe. He finished washing as quickly as he could and stepped out.

He heard the boom several times that night. Vaguely, he remembered his parents discussing the drainpipes in the house. There was something different about them. In the morning, Jeremy asked his mom, "Where does the water go when we flush?"

"The septic tank," his mom said.

"Not the sewer?" Jeremy asked.

His mom shook her head. "We don't have sewers here. The houses are too far apart. Everything goes into a big tank. Then it decomposes, and the water filters out into the ground. There's a special bacteria in there that breaks stuff down."

Jeremy was listening to her, but in the background, far away, he heard the boom again. *No*, he realized, it wasn't far away. It was up close, but buried underground. That's why it seemed distant.

It was right next to the house.

Jeremy wondered what form of life could possible grow in there—grow large enough to pound with such force. He shuddered as his mind ran through a dozen dark and slimy images. The most awful of them was the most familiar—something shaped just like him. Manlike, but far from human.

His mother was still talking. She'd mentioned something about a pump, but Jeremy hadn't caught it. Now, she was talking about clogged drains. "We can't even use drain cleaner," she explained. "It would kill the bacteria. I can't have a garbage disposal, either, but that's really not a problem since . . ."

Jeremy tuned her out. He didn't care about pumps or disposals. But drain cleaner—now that was a different story. That was nasty stuff. He wondered where he could find some. "Got it," he said to himself. Down in the basement there was a bunch of boxes that hadn't been unpacked after the move last year.

His parents never threw anything out. Jeremy could just see his father grabbing the drain cleaner and saying, "Who knows? We might be able to use it some day." Then he'd throw it in a box along with half-empty cans of hardened paint, parts for a car he no longer owned, and a microphone from a tape recorder that had broken four or five years ago.

It took a half hour of searching, but Jeremy knew the bottle as soon as he saw it. CAUTION—KEEP OUT OF REACH OF CHILDREN, it read in big red letters. WARNING—CAUSES IRREVERSIBLE EYE DAMAGE. HARMFUL OR FATAL IF SWALLOWED. Best of all, the bottle felt nearly full.

Jeremy took the drain cleaner over to the sink in the laundry room. He started to open it, then looked again at the words on the label. "No point in me getting hurt," he said. He grabbed his mother's gardening gloves. Then he found the safety glasses his father used when he sprayed bug killer on the trees.

As Jeremy opened the cap, he paused for a moment. The part of him that had been told to be kind and thoughtful, to avoid being mean or cruel, that part of him whispered thoughts of peace and mercy. The whispers were drowned out by a thudding, pounding pulse from outside. Jeremy shook his head. There would be no mercy.

"Have a nice bath." Jeremy dumped the entire bottle of drain cleaner into the sink. As it swirled down the drain, the fumes burned his nose.

Jeremy turned on the water to wash all the drain cleaner into the septic tank. "There," he said. "That should take care of you."

As he walked away from the laundry room, he heard one loud thud echo through the pipes. Then, faintly, a roar of pain.

Then silence.

Jeremy went upstairs, knowing he'd beaten whatever beast lived in the tank. There was no more pounding that day, or the next.

But there was a faint odor drifting through the house, as if someone across the room had unpeeled a hard-boiled egg. Jeremy noticed his father sniffing the air. His parents talked about the problem. Then his father searched through the phone book and made a call.

The next day, Jeremy looked out his bedroom window and saw a large truck drive to the side of the house. He heard a man talking to his parents.

After he got dressed, Jeremy wandered into the backyard. There was a fresh hole near the rear corner of the house on the side away from the road. The man had a long, thick hose running from the truck to the hole.

"What are you doing?" Jeremy asked.

"Pumping the septic tank," the man said.

Jeremy moved next to the man and looked down. About a foot beneath the ground, he saw a large opening. The cover for the opening—a round slab of concrete, shaped like a manhole cover—was off to the side.

A deep, rotting smell rose from the hole. Jeremy wondered what would be revealed when the tank was pumped. He wanted to see the creature he'd destroyed.

"Do you pump out everything?" he asked.

"As much as we can," the man said, "but if—" He stopped talking as the hose jerked. "What in the world . . . ?" he said, picking up the hose from the ground.

The man looked at the hose, then back at the truck. "It can't be clogged. No way . . ." He looked back down toward the hole and wiggled the hose back and forth.

The hose jerked again. This time it was yanked forward. The man stumbled against the pull. He bumped into Jeremy.

Jeremy staggered and took a step that ended in emptiness.

Jeremy fell.

Unimaginably, unbearably, he plunged into the half-empty pit of decomposing sewage.

He grabbed for the hose, his eyes squeezed tightly shut against the stench that washed around him, his stomach churning in disgust beyond anything he had ever imagined.

He wanted to scream, but he didn't dare open his mouth.

His hand met the hose. He grabbed on and started to pull himself up to the world of clean air and pure water.

It was easy. Like climbing a rope in gym class.

The roar, unmuffled by the cushion of soil and cement and pipes, was deafening in the chamber of the septic tank. The roar was followed by a splash as something massive burst from beneath the surface behind him. Jeremy froze as a huge arm wrapped around his chest and yanked him from the hose.

In an instant, he was dragged down and swallowed by the murk. He clawed at the slimy arm, but it was far too strong. There was no chance of escape.

Just as Jeremy was about to give up all hope, the arm loosened for a moment, as if the creature was considering mercy. Jeremy nearly cried out in relief. He remembered his own brief pause, his hesitation before pouring the drain cleaner.

Then the grip tightened again.

No sign of mercy from below.

No sign of Jeremy from above.

ANYTHING YOU WANT

If I'd found the bottle, I'd be sitting on a mountain of chocolate right now. I'd be counting my billion dollars right now. That's right—I'd be counting my billion dollars, eating my chocolate, and flying around the world with the aid of my superpowers.

But Stevie found the bottle.

Not only that, he found it when I was with him, so I got to watch him make his stupid wishes, and that was even worse.

Stevie's three, which is part of the problem. Mom stuck me with him for the afternoon. We went to the park and took a walk through Sherman's Woods. It's not really a woods—just a bunch of trees that happened to be in the same area. There weren't as many trees as usual. A big windstorm had swept through town last night, knocking over stuff like trees, phone poles, and small cars.

"Look!" Stevie shouted as we walked through the woods. He ran over to a fallen tree. The roots had been pulled from the ground and were spread out like a real bad hairdo that had been combed by a nervous stylist. Stevie reached down under the roots. "Look, Sissie, look!" He calls me that because I'm his sister and he has a hard time saying Rebecca.

"Careful," I warned him. I could just see him getting his finger chomped by a gopher or muskrat, or whatever lived under the ground.

"Pretty," Stevie said, holding something up. That's basically how he talks—one word at a time, sometimes two or three words. But I wasn't thinking about language—I was looking at what Stevie had found.

"Wow. Let me see." I walked over and held my hand out.

"Mine," Stevie said. He clutched the bottle close to his chest. From the glimpse I'd gotten, I knew it was something unusual. It was made out of shiny metal, and there were jewels all around it.

"Come on, just let me see it . . ."

Stevie shook his head. "Bottle mine."

That's when the bottle glowed. It shined so brightly, the metal seemed almost like glass. Then the cork popped out and this burst of steam shot up.

The steam turned into a genie.

I knew he was a genie because he looked at Stevie and said, "I grant thee three wishes."

"Wishes?" Stevie asked.

"Stevie, let me tell you what to ask for." I was sure a kid his age would get the wrong things. Not me. I could make perfect wishes.

"Silence!" the genie said, glaring at me.

I wasn't going to argue. His eyes had that same look Mom

and Dad get before they stop trying to reason with me and send me to my room.

"Make your wishes, mortal," the genie said to Stevie. "You may have anything your heart desires."

Wouldn't you know it? When he could have anything in the world, what does Stevie do? My brilliant younger brother opens his mouth and asks for his favorite food. "Peas," he told the genie. "Want peas."

Yuk. I shook my head. This was disgusting. Stevie loved those peas that come in the can—the soft, squishy ones that are the color of old paint. Mom makes them for him almost every night. I wondered how many peas the genie would give him. I could almost see him being buried in tons of peas while the genie laughed.

But, apparently, this wasn't that kind of genie. I found that out right away. I also found out that I can understand Stevie a lot better than other people—or genies.

"A noble wish," the genie said. "I have not granted such a request in many centuries. You have asked for peace, and I will grant you peace. The whole world will know a period of peace. No wars for one hundred years." He closed his eyes for a moment, then opened them and said, "It is done."

"Peas?" Stevie asked, looking around.

I could tell he was disappointed.

"Your next wish?" the genie asked.

"Liver," Stevie said, shaking his head. "Never."

I groaned. He was wishing that Mom would never make liver again. What a waste. All he had to do was feed it to the dog like I did.

But I guess Stevie really didn't speak very clearly this time, either. The genie said, "Very well, you shall live forever." He closed his eyes again, then opened them and said, "It is done."

I couldn't stand it. I had to say something. "Careful, Stevie, this is your last wish. Don't waste it."

The genie glared at me again. "Sorry," I said, very quietly. I tried to guess what Stevie would wish for next. It could be anything. And there was no way to know what the genie would think Stevie said.

Before Stevie could open his mouth, I tried to catch his attention. I waved my hand, making sure the genie didn't see. It worked. Stevie looked at me and smiled. I smiled back. I think Stevie got the idea.

He looked up at the genie and said, "Sissie wish."

Phew. Good job, Stevie, I thought. He'd asked the genie to give me his last wish. Well, it was just one out of three, but I figured that was better than nothing.

The genie frowned for a moment, like he wasn't sure he'd heard correctly. Then he said, "Very well, I will make your sister a fish."

He closed his eyes.

"Wait!" I shouted.

The next thing I knew, I was flopping on the ground, gasping for breath. At least Stevie knew enough to pick me up and toss me into the stream.

So now I'm a fish. That's the bad part. But I don't have to watch Stevie anymore. That's the good part. All in all, I guess it worked out about even.

LINE**ſ**

Stay in line, please," Mrs. Epstein shouted as her students shuffled down the hallway toward their music class.

Andrea, walking in the other direction after running an errand for her teacher, Mr. Sutcliff, smiled as she passed the squirming, shoving gang of kids. She remembered her own days in Mrs. Epstein's kindergarten. The little kids always seemed to be lining up. Whatever they did, wherever they went, they went in a line.

It hasn't changed, Andrea realized. Even now that she was older, she still spent so much time going from place to place in a line. It wasn't quite as bad as back then, but there still were so many lines.

She reached her class just in time to hear Mr. Sutcliff say, "Okay kids, line up. We're going to the auditorium to see a film."

Andrea got into line with the others. But as soon as the line started moving down the hall, she stepped aside and waited for her friend Nichole to reach her. Then she started walking along next to Nichole.

"Hey," Nichole asked, "what are you doing?"

"Going to the auditorium," Andrea told her.

"But you aren't in line," Nichole said. She looked ahead as if checking to see whether Mr. Sutcliff had noticed.

Andrea shrugged. "So? I don't see what the big deal is. I'll still get there, right? I'm not making trouble. I'm not doing anything bad. I'm just not in the line. Do you really care?"

Nichole didn't answer.

"Okay, be like that," Andrea said. "But I'm not getting into the line."

She walked next to Nichole as they went to the end of the side hall and turned into the front hall that led to the auditorium. Mr. Sutcliff looked back at the line as the last of the kids came around the corner.

Andrea was a little surprised. She figured that her teacher would say something. But he didn't.

"See," Andrea said when the front of the line had reached the auditorium. "Nothing bad happened."

Nichole didn't even look at her.

"In you go, kids," Mr. Sutcliff said. "One, two, three, four," he counted as the class filed into the auditorium. He was a compulsive counter. Andrea couldn't help thinking of the Count on *Sesame Street* every time Mr. Sutcliff began numbering the students.

Nichole started to go through the door. "Wait up," Andrea said.

Her friend didn't even look over.

"Come on, don't be like that." Andrea reached out and pushed Nichole's shoulder.

Her hand went through her friend as if one of them wasn't real.

Andrea froze.

"Eighteen, nineteen, and twenty makes everyone," Mr. Sutcliff said as the last of the students went through the door.

"It's just a line," Andrea said weakly. She realized she was fading. She'd fallen out of the system when she stepped out of the line. Andrea watched the auditorium door drift shut.

There was only one chance. She waited. When the film was over, the students filed out. Andrea joined the line, walking behind Nichole, who was the last one to leave.

With each step, she felt a bit more solid. As she passed down the familiar halls, she felt reality grow firm again. This was her school. This was where she belonged. This was her line.

As they reached the classroom and broke the line, Andrea tapped Nichole's shoulder.

Solid flesh.

"Hi," Nichole said, turning and smiling.

"Hi," Andrea said back, feeling a relief beyond anything she could describe. That had been close. But she'd escaped disaster.

"You like it here?" Nichole asked.

"What?" Andrea didn't know what she was talking about.

"You're the new girl, right?" Nichole asked. "You must have just moved here. I don't think we've met yet. My name's Nichole. Hey, maybe we can be friends. Want to come over to my house after school?"

Andrea nodded and wondered what else she'd lost when she'd stepped out of the line.

WANDERING STU

MINE!" Stuart screamed, ripping the baseball out of his little brother's hands. "It's mine. Get your own baseball."

Billy ran into the house, crying hard enough to drown his sneakers. Stuart stood clutching the ball for a moment, then dropped it back on the lawn where it had been lying before Billy picked it up. He didn't want to play with it at the moment—he just didn't want someone else to play with it. After all, it was *his* ball.

Stuart turned to go inside, but his path was blocked by the stranger.

"One thousand times," the stranger said.

Stuart took a step back. "Get off my property. You're trespassing. My dad has a gun. You'd better get going."

The man didn't seem to care about Stuart's dad's imaginary gun. "One thousand days of uninterrupted selfishness," the stranger said. "Not one break. Not one single day when you didn't act as if you were the only person living on this planet. Congratulations, Stuart. That's a record."

"Record?" Stuart asked, suddenly interested in hearing more from the stranger. "Did I win a prize or something?"

The stranger nodded. "Indeed you did." He raised his arms and clapped his hands together.

Stuart shut his eyes as a bright flash filled the air. When he looked, all he could do for a moment was stare. His house had vanished.

"Hey!" Stuart shouted. "What did you do with my house?"

"Mine, mine, mine," the stranger said. "See? That's all you ever think about. You need to learn to think about other people. You need to be taught a lesson."

"But I—"

Before Stuart could finish his sentence, the stranger vanished, just like the house.

"Might as well go over to Joey's house," Stuart muttered as he walked down the block. He didn't really like Joey, but he hung out there sometimes because Joey's mother was always buying big bags of candy.

There was nobody home at Joey's house. But the door was open. Stuart went in and grabbed a sack of Snickers. Then he wandered down the block.

There was nobody in any of the houses.

Stuart wandered into town. He didn't find a single person. But that was fine with him. He ran wild through the mall, playing with all the cool stuff in the sporting goods stores, trying the drums in the music store, and checking out all the new video games in the game store.

It was fun. For a while.

After several days, Stuart started to get bored.

"Hey!" he called. "Where are you?" He figured that any-one who could make his house disappear could probably hear him, too.

"Yes?" the stranger asked, popping out of the air in front of him.

"Look," Stuart said. "You made your point. I've been self-ish. That's what this is all about. Right?"

"Right," the stranger said.

"I acted like I was the only person on the planet. So that's what you did. You made me the only one here—for real."

The stranger grinned. "Pretty fitting, wouldn't you say?"

"Yeah. Great. I have to admire you. Really wonderful," Stuart said. "So like what do I have to do to get things back the way they were? I mean, I realized that I've been selfish. I'm cured. I learned my lesson. Isn't that enough?"

"Almost," the stranger said. "But to return your world to the way it was, you must do one thing. Now that you realize the error of your ways, it won't be a problem. It's a very sim-ple thing."

"So tell me," Stuart said. He was running out of patience.

The stranger grinned. "All you have to do is perform one totally unselfish deed. You need to do something nice for . . ." The grin fell from the stranger's face. He stopped talking.

"Do something nice for who?" Stuart asked. He was ready. He was willing. He figured he could do one nice deed with-out suffering too much.

"For someone," the stranger said. He looked away from Stuart.

"For someone?" Stuart asked. "But you took everyone away. So how can I do something nice for someone?"

"Oops," the stranger said. His voice grew so quiet it was close to a whisper. He shook his head. "Sorry. I'm kinda new at this."

"So bring them back," Stuart said.

The stranger shook his head. "I can't. It doesn't work that way. Once the conditions are set, they have to be met. Hey—that rhymed. It has to be like that, to prevent cheating. Sorry, I don't make the rules."

"But I can't help someone if there's nobody to help. Can I do something for you?" Stuart asked. "That would work, right?"

"Nope. Doesn't count. Well, I'd better get going. No point in my staying here."

"Wait!" Stuart said.

"Sorry. Good luck. Hope you figure something out." The stranger clapped his hands together and vanished.

Stuart wandered down the street, alone.

TARNATION

My bedroom is over the garage. I have to share the room with my wimpy dork of a brother, Alexander. He's only five. It's not a lot of fun sharing a room, especially since Alexander can't sleep through the night without getting up at least a couple billion times to go to the bathroom. Which wouldn't be all that bad except that he has to put the light on before he'll stick his nose into the hall. That's because he's worried about running into a monster.

"There aren't any monsters," I told him one night before we went to sleep. I was getting really tired of waking up every time he turned on the light.

"Yes, there are," he said. "Billy Morrison in my kindergarten told me you can call monsters. They'll come to your house. Honest. But they only come at night."

"Why would you want to call a monster?" I asked.

"If they like you, they'll give you a present," Alexander said.

"Yeah, sure. And what if they don't like you?" I asked.

"Billy didn't say."

I laughed at him. Then I forgot all about it. He was always babbling about crazy junk he'd heard from other kids. It's amazing what those kids in kindergarten will believe.

I was sitting at my desk the next day, doing my homework, when Alexander came in and said, "I found out the monster stuff from Billy."

"Yeah. Okay. Tell me later." I was more interested in looking out the window at what Dad was doing. Every fall, he spread this thick, sticky gunk on the driveway, fixing all the cracks. We couldn't walk on it until it dried. That took a day. I didn't see what the big deal was about having a perfect driveway, but I guess it was important to Dad.

"Can we do the monster stuff?" Alexander asked.

"Not right now," I told him. "I've got homework."

"Later?"

"Sure." I'd promise him anything to get him to shut up.

Naturally, he didn't forget my promise. "Can we try the monster stuff?" he asked right after I went to bed.

"Go to sleep."

"You promised."

"Just go to sleep."

"YOU PROMISED!"

"Okay, okay. Don't wake Mom and Dad." The way he was shouting, I was afraid the folks would come running into the room. Their bedroom was on the other side of the house, and they were both pretty sound sleepers, but there was something about Alexander's shouts that could wake up just about anyone. "What do we have to do."

"Just say *Monster, monster, come to me.*"

"That's all?" It sounded a bit too easy.

"We have to say it a hundred times."

"No way." This was getting ridiculous.

"YOU PROMISED!"

"Shut up, okay? I'll do it. Let's get started." I have to admit, there was a part of me that wondered how long it would take to say something one hundred times. It was a bit cool to think about that. I realized I could keep track with my fingers. I could use them to count to ten, and Alexander could use his fingers to count groups of ten.

I turned on the light, then explained to him that every time I held up all ten fingers, he had to stick out one more of his fingers. He accepted what I was saying almost as if it was another part of the magic.

"That will be a hundred?" he asked.

"Yeah. Ten groups of ten. Like if you have ten pennies, that's a dime. And ten dimes make a dollar."

"But that's not a hundred dimes," he said.

"Just trust me."

"Okay."

"By the way, what kind of present does the monster bring?" I asked.

Alexander shrugged. "Billy didn't say. But the more the monster likes you, the better the present. I'll bet we get something really good."

We started. I figured the sooner we got it over with, the sooner Alexander would leave me alone.

Monster, monster, come to me.

I kept count. At ten, I wiggled my fingers. It took Alexander a second, but he caught on and held out his right thumb.

At first, it seemed to go quickly. But by the thirtieth time, my throat was getting a bit dry. We made it past fifty, then reached seventy. I couldn't believe it was that hard. By ninety, I could barely speak. Alexander's voice was the merest croak. I would have given anything for a glass of water. I wanted to stop. But there was another part of me that didn't want to give up. It had nothing to do with Alexander's stupid kindergarten magic—I wanted to do it just so I could say I'd done it.

Monster, monster, come to me.

We got to ninety-five. I wanted to cough or clear my throat.

Then ninety-six. I felt that any extra sound—a cough or anything else—would ruin everything. I didn't even dare clear my throat.

Monster, monster, come to me.

Ninety-seven. This was crazy. Why was I doing this? My whole mouth was so dry I thought it was going to crack wide open.

Monster, monster, come to me.

Ninety-eight.

Monster, monster, come to me.

Ninety-nine. I fought back the urge to cough. I looked at Alexander. He was struggling, too.

Monster, monster, come to me.

One hundred.

We both stopped. The room seemed dead quiet. I looked at Alexander. He looked at me.

He was the first to speak. "Bet it's a great present."

I was about to open my mouth and say, "Don't be silly." But I wasn't sure if I could talk. And the shriek came before I could speak.

It came from outside—from below our room. I ran to the window. Out in the driveway, something struggled and howled. A face, the most awful and angry face I'd ever seen, glared up from below as the monster struggled to free itself from the sticky tar in the driveway.

The howls lasted through most of the night. I tried holding the pillow over my ears. It helped some, but I still knew it was out there. Alexander was so scared, he crawled into my bed. For once, he didn't get up to go to the bathroom. Neither of us wanted to look out the window. I didn't need to look—I'd never be able to get that face out of my mind. It was like a giant lizard had gotten too close to a firecracker right when it went off. It was all green and red and twisted and wet.

At some point, before sunrise, I think the howling stopped. I guess I finally fell asleep.

When I awoke, I was confused for a moment. Why was Alexander in my bed? Why was my throat so dry and sore? Then it all came back to me. I sat up. Alexander sat up.

"Was it real?" he asked.

"I don't know." I ran to the window. There was no sign of the monster. Maybe it had been a dream. Maybe we'd fallen asleep while saying those stupid words.

That's when Dad started shouting for us. He called us both downstairs and made us walk out to the driveway. He sounded really angry. "Who's responsible for this?" he asked, pointing to a spot beneath the bedroom window.

I looked where he pointed. There was something stuck to the tar—something that looked like lizard skin. There were two torn pieces. For a moment, I thought they were just formless blobs. Then, with a jolt, I realized they were roughly in the shape of huge footprints.

"When I find out who did this," Dad said, "someone is going to be sorry."

Not as sorry as we're going to be tonight, I thought. Alexander had said that the monster would bring presents if it liked us. Tonight, there would be no fresh tar to stop it. I wondered what a monster did when it didn't like you. I wondered what it did when it was really unhappy with you.

Tonight, I'll say *Monster, monster, stay away*. I'll make Alexander say it, too. We'll say it a hundred times. We'll say it a thousand times. We'll say it every night, if we get the chance.

TEN POUNDS OF CHOCOLATE

No way," Amy said. "That can't be true."

"I swear," Wendy said. "She gives out huge chocolate bars. My brother told me."

Amy looked down the hill. The house had to be a half mile away. But at least it was downhill. "You sure about this?"

Wendy nodded.

"Okay. If it's true, it'll be worth the trip." Amy headed down the hill, hitching up her skirt. The witch costume was great, but it was just a bit too long.

There weren't any other homes to stop at along the way—just empty lots filled with tall weeds. Amy hoped she wasn't wasting her time.

"My turn to ring," Wendy said when they reached the house. At least the front light was on. She rushed to the porch.

Amy followed her up the creaking steps and waited for the door to open. The place was small—little more than a cabin—and it didn't seem to be in very good condition. Amy wondered how anyone who lived here could afford to give away big bars of chocolate to every kid who came by.

"Well, aren't you two just lovely," the woman said when she opened the door. She was old and small, just like the house. Behind her, a black cat peered at the girls, its tail forming question marks in the air.

"Trick or—" Amy started to say. But the words caught in her throat as she spotted what lay on the table in the hallway. Two huge candy bars—the biggest she'd ever seen. Maybe Wendy was right. The bars looked like they weighed at least ten pounds each.

"Here you go, dearie," the woman said. She stooped and lifted a candy bar with two hands, then dropped it into Amy's bag.

Amy felt her arm jolt as the weight hit. "Thank you," she said. She could already taste the chocolate. It would last for weeks.

"And here you go, young lady," the woman said, giving the other bar to Wendy.

Lucky us, Amy thought, realizing she and her friend had gotten the last two candy bars.

"That's very generous," Wendy said.

The woman nodded. "An old person like me needs to be extra friendly. I'm all alone here except for Jackson," she said, pointing to the cat. "I want people to think well of me. That way, they won't play tricks on me or make up nasty rumors."

Amy nodded. It made sense. The woman was alone in

this tiny house at the end of a long road. If she didn't give out candy on Halloween, some of the kids might do bad things to her property. But if she gave out great candy, she'd never have a problem.

"Thanks again," Amy said as the girls left the house.

"Come back next year," the woman called.

"Wow, that was worth the trip." Amy started the long climb up the hill.

"And even worth the trip back," Wendy added.

"Ten pounds at least," Amy said. She lifted the candy bar from her bag.

"Yeah." Wendy hefted her own bar. "It must cost her a fortune to buy these. But I guess she really wants kids to like her. I know I'm going to tell everyone how nice she is."

"Me, too." Amy was about to put the candy bar back in her bag when she heard the roar. She froze for an instant. "What was that?"

"Just some kids fooling around," Wendy said, though she didn't sound very sure.

Amy hitched up her skirt and walked faster. Another roar ripped the air, closer this time. Amy looked back and screamed as the dark beast leaped from the tall weeds, sprinting toward them on four legs and spitting out a fierce and angry growl. Its sharp white teeth glistened like ivory daggers.

"Run!" she shouted.

Amy dashed up the hill. The chocolate bar felt heavier and heavier. It became an anchor, threatening to drag her to a halt. She dropped the bar and ran harder. By her side, she saw Wendy toss her own bar to the ground.

At the top of the hill, Amy paused and looked back. "We made it," she gasped, trying to catch her breath. "What was that? A wolf? A lion?"

Wendy shook her head. "I don't know. But I lost my candy bar."

Amy nodded. "Me, too. But at least we got away. And we still have our bags." She was beginning to wonder if it had been her imagination. But she knew one thing for certain. "She sure is a nice old lady."

"Yeah," Wendy said. "She's really nice."

Amy saw two boys walk past, heading down the hill. She opened her mouth to warn them about the beast, but then decided not to say anything. They wouldn't believe her. And she couldn't blame them. There couldn't really have been a creature chasing them.

"Come on," Wendy said. "Let's go to some more houses." She walked away from the hill.

"Good idea." Amy followed her.

At that same moment, down at the bottom of the hill, the sleek, black panther opened his jaws and gently placed the two huge chocolate bars on the porch of the small house. Then he clawed at the door, his waving tail forming question marks in the air.

"Well done, Jackson. We've made so many friends tonight," the nice old woman said. She picked up the chocolate bars, one by one, and placed them back on the table, then petted the panther as it again took the form of a cat. "And just in time," she added, peering up the hill. "I believe I see more youngsters heading our way."

THE BOY WHO WOULDN'T TALK

None of us knew how Tommy Griffin got away with it, but he never talked. I don't mean that he didn't say very much. I don't mean that he rarely spoke. I mean he *never* talked. We were pretty sure he was able to talk, though not everyone agreed about that. We'd discussed the whole thing many times.

"Maybe there's something wrong with his throat," Arnie said one day last March when we were hanging out at the playground after lunch.

"No way," Shawn said. "He'd use sign language or something if that's all the problem was."

I nodded. I'd seen a few of his test grades when the papers were handed back. He was solidly there in the B+ to A− range. If he *couldn't* talk, he'd have some other way to communicate. "I don't think he can't talk," I told them. "I think he won't talk."

"Why?" Shawn asked.

"Maybe something awful happened to him," Arnie said.

"You know, something so terrible, he lost his voice. Maybe he was in a horrible accident. Yeah, that's got to be the answer. I'll bet the teachers know about it, and that's why they don't make him speak in class."

This explanation was our favorite. But, that day, it wasn't enough for me. That day, I had to open my big mouth. "I don't know what the reason is, but I'm going to find out." I'd already tried asking him. We'd all tried at least a couple of times. But Tommy just kind of half-smiled and shrugged like he didn't understand the question.

Once, about a month after Tommy showed up at the school last year, Kent, who is about the worst bully in the class, threatened him. "Say something or I'll pound you," Kent had shouted. Tommy stood there looking at him. He didn't move a muscle; he didn't blink. I don't know what went through Kent's head, but he just muttered, "It ain't worth the effort," and walked off, leaving the crowd without their taste of blood.

I didn't get off so easily when I bragged that I'd find out the reason. Everyone jumped all over me. "Yeah, right," Shawn said.

"Sure," Arnie said. "He'll talk to you. Yup."

They were laughing and snickering. What could I do? It had become a matter of pride. I followed Tommy Griffin home that day. I stayed far enough behind so he wouldn't spot me. It wasn't hard. He never looked back. He just walked along with those funny little steps of his, going straight down the middle of the sidewalk. He was one strange kid.

I kept pretending I was some sort of super-detective. At

first, it was fun. After a while, I began to understand where the term "flatfoot" came from. We just kept on walking—Tommy went along without a clue that I was there, and I followed him without a clue where we were going. If I hadn't boasted in front of all my friends, I would have just turned around and gone home. I realized there was at least one big advantage to not talking—you didn't get stuck having to do what you said you'd do.

We must have gone a couple miles. The neighborhood started to change. It happened slowly. One house needed a paint job. Another was missing some shutters over the windows. One farther down was missing windows. Then the changes came more quickly.

I started to feel uncomfortable. It didn't look like anybody lived around here. *Enough of this*, I thought. So what if everyone kidded me. They'd forget about it soon enough. I was about to give up and head for home when Tommy finally moved from the center of the sidewalk. He turned, walked through an opening in a fence where the front gate had rusted off, and went up five warped wooden steps into a small house at the end of a row of small houses. There wasn't a sign of another person anywhere.

Now what? I walked past the house and around the corner. The fence ran along the side, but it had several large holes near the bottom. I could see a yard in the back. It was almost all dirt—just one or two small patches of dying grass. I ducked through one of the holes and crawled into the yard.

What would I say if he came out? "Hi, Tommy, just

wanted to drop by for a chat." Yeah, that would fool him for sure. I just hoped he hadn't seen me.

There were two windows in the back on the first floor. I went up to one and tried to look through. It was so dirty it might as well have been made of slate. I tried another. It was a bit better. There was movement inside the house. I found a corner of the glass that wasn't as dirty as the rest and peered into Tommy's world.

He was facing away from me, standing in front of this large box. It was about six inches high, and about six feet on a side, like a big sandbox. It looked like it was filled with dirt. Tommy stepped up into it, then stretched out his arms and flopped forward.

He just lay there, facedown in the dirt.

Slowly, Tommy changed. His fingers grew longer. Oh man, I didn't believe what I was seeing. Tommy was growing into the soil. His feet were bare. His toes burrowed into the ground, too.

I must have watched for at least an hour. I wanted to run, but I had to see. Tommy was no longer recognizable as human in any sense. His body, the middle part, was still on top of the soil, but his arms and legs and head had sunk into the earth.

I had to get out of there. This was all too weird. I started to take a step away.

I couldn't.

Something was clutching my foot. I looked down. A thick vine had come up from the ground by my feet and wrapped around my ankle. It had caught me.

Tommy had caught me.

———

I never talk in school. I could, I guess, if I wanted to. But I have nothing in common with these flesh creatures, these children and teachers. It's not a problem. My mind is very strong, and they bend to my will. I'm not lonely. I talk with Tommy every night. We have a lot to say to each other. A whole lot. We talk and we plan, and we decide who will join us next.

INVASION OF THE ROAD WEENIES

As the school bus rattled down the road, Marlon looked out the window and spotted a jogger coming toward him. The guy was wearing blue shorts, a sweat-streaked white T-shirt, and a red baseball cap. When the bus reached the man, Marlon noticed something else. The jogger was frowning.

"They never smile," Marlon said.

"Who?" Hector asked.

"The joggers." Marlon turned toward his seatmate. "Have you ever seen one smile?"

"Guess not," Hector said. "So?"

"I don't know. But what's the point if it isn't fun? They always look like they're hurting themselves."

Hector shrugged and zipped open his backpack, reached in, pulled out his homework, then shoved it back in. That drove Marlon crazy. Every day, Hector would check his pack a dozen times during the ride.

"It's not going to vanish," Marlon said.

"I just want to make sure it's there," Hector said. He let out a nervous laugh. "Seeing is believing."

On the way to school, Marlon saw three more joggers. Different ages, different clothes, but the same pained expression. He started thinking of them as road weenies—mindless, grim-faced creatures who puffed and gasped all over town for reasons nobody would ever know.

During class, while looking out a window from the second floor, Marlon noticed another jogger slogging along the road that ran past the school. Marlon had a hard time telling from the distance, but he was pretty sure this jogger wasn't smiling, either.

On the long bus ride home—Marlon's was the next to last stop—he spotted four more joggers. No smiles. And, odder yet, no familiar faces.

I don't know any of them, Marlon realized as he got off the bus. He'd lived in Lynchville all his life and knew most of his neighbors, but there wasn't a single familiar face among the joggers.

That night, Marlon drew a rough map of the town in his notebook. At the top of the map, he wrote *RW* for road weenies. The next morning, he marked the spot where he saw each jogger. He used initials: *RH* for the guy with the red hat, *BB* for the guy with the black beard, *SV* for the woman with the sun visor, and so on. The bus was often a couple minutes early or late, depending on traffic. So Marlon saw the joggers at slightly different times each day. From where they were on the road, he was able to figure out part of each jogger's path.

Marlon spent three weeks gathering all the information. When he was done, he discovered that the map revealed a secret. *They cover every single road in town*, he thought. Each day, the joggers ran over every mile of roadway.

On Sunday, Marlon got on his bike, ducked into the tall weeds in a gully along Locust Street, and waited for a jogger to pass. It didn't take long. Marlon watched until the man was far ahead. Then he climbed out of his hiding place and pedaled slowly behind, keeping back where he wouldn't be spotted.

The man jogged all the way to the end of Locust, then turned south on Bryar. He covered half of Bryar, all of Elm, and the eastern part of Flagler. Finally, he disappeared into an old barn at the edge of town.

Marlon was about to pedal closer when another jogger came along. This one also slipped into the barn. Marlon stayed back and watched. As the morning passed, five more joggers showed up and went inside. Three joggers left the barn, but they were different people—not the same ones who had come in that morning.

Finally, as curiosity overwhelmed caution, Marlon took a chance and sneaked toward the barn from the side opposite the door. He knelt by the wall, then crept around the corner and moved along until he reached a spot below a small window. Holding his breath, Marlon stood and peeked inside.

The barn was filled with men and women. Marlon recognized some of the joggers he'd seen. They were all just standing there in a line. As Marlon watched, another jogger came through the door. He walked to the rear of the line. A jogger at the other end walked to the door, then loped out.

As each jogger returned, another left. This continued until the sun began to set. Then, as the rest came in, nobody else went out to replace them. By dark, they were all inside, standing motionless. The last jogger to return was a man with red jogging shorts and a white T-shirt. He walked up and down the line once, as if he was in charge, and then took his place at the back.

Marlon crept quietly around to the front of the barn. He found a stick and slid it through the handles on the double doors, locking them closed.

That night, in bed, Marlon wondered what he hoped to accomplish. He wasn't sure why he'd locked the joggers inside. Maybe to help figure out what was going on.

He didn't see any joggers the next morning.

"Weird," Hector said as they rode toward school. "I just got these glasses." He pulled them off and squinted in the direction of the window. Then he wiped the glasses with the bottom of his shirt and put them back on. "They seemed fine last night. Do the trees look out of focus to you?"

"Nope." Marlon wasn't really listening to Hector. He was busy staring out the window, wondering what had happened after he'd locked the barn door.

I'll go to the barn after school, he told himself. But he was halfway afraid to go back.

The next morning, the world was a little blurry when Marlon got up. On the way to school, he blinked and stared through the window of the bus, looking for joggers. There weren't any.

"I don't remember everything ever being so fuzzy," Hector said. "Something is definitely different."

That night, Marlon went to the barn.

He pulled out the stick and opened the door. The joggers were inside, standing the way he'd left them. "Come on," he called. "Get out there. Come on. Jog!"

They didn't move. Marlon stared out the door at the blurry, dim land around him. The world looked like a faded memory.

Faded memory . . . Something seen once, but slowly forgotten. Maybe seeing was even more than believing. Maybe seeing was all that kept things real. Most people never bothered to look at the world. They were too busy talking or playing. But the joggers—all they did was stare ahead.

Marlon started to jog, running the map of town through his head, wondering how long it would take him to cover every street and see every part of town. How long would it take to freshen the memory?

It took all night. But in the morning, as he reached the barn, finishing the circuit, the world seemed more real.

When Marlon opened the door, the man in the red shorts was waiting for him, along with the other joggers. "Glad you could join us," the man said. "You'd better get going. It's time to start today's run." He told Marlon what route to take.

"But . . ." Marlon was exhausted from jogging all night.

"Get going," the man said. His voice had turned cold.

Marlon started jogging up the road. He didn't smile.

WE INTERRUPT THIS
PROGRAM

Kids notice things that adults never see. That's how I found the INSERT button on the TV remote control. When my folks are home from work, my dad does the channel surfing, so he uses the remote a lot in the evening. But after school, I usually have the TV all to myself for about an hour. Then my stepbrother Harold gets home and takes away the remote.

I was sitting there one afternoon, trying to find something worth watching, when I ran my finger along the side of the remote control. Instead of a smooth edge, I felt a seam. I tore my eyes from the TV—it was an old western movie—and looked at the remote. Sure enough, the front was in two pieces. I pushed and pulled at the bottom until a piece slid open. It was like a battery compartment, but I knew the battery went in the back. This front compartment just held two buttons: INSERT and REMOVE.

Not giving it any special thought, I pressed INSERT. In a flash, there were cowboys all around me. They were trying to control a cattle stampede. There were also cows all around. I'd inserted myself into the program.

Usually, I don't think very fast, but some instinct made me press REMOVE.

I was back in the living room. This was interesting.

For the next week, I went in and out of hundreds of places. The cartoons were the coolest, but they could be pretty dangerous. I thought I was in big trouble the time I jumped in just when Wile E. Coyote was setting off a bomb. But it was a cartoon bomb, so it didn't hurt me. It felt strange. I can't really describe it except that it was like being clobbered by tons of whipped cream.

Then, I made a mistake. I was having so much fun riding a raft down this wild river that I lost track of time. At the end of the trip, I hit REMOVE and popped back to the couch just as Harold was walking in the room.

"Hey, how'd you do that?"

"Do what?" I asked, sliding the compartment closed.

Harold grabbed the front of my shirt and yanked me off the couch. "Do you want me to make you tell?"

What could I do? I knew I'd still have an hour to myself, even if Harold took over each day when he got home. Besides, if I didn't tell him, he'd twist my arm real bad. I showed him the button.

"Thanks. Now get out of here." Harold grabbed the remote and turned back to the TV. He started surfing the channels. I guess he was looking for somewhere exciting to go for his first time. He kept passing by stuff, saying, "No fun," "Boring," or "Give me a break."

Finally, he stopped. "That's more like it."

I looked at his choice. "I don't think that's a good idea."

"I didn't ask you," he said.

"But—"

He pushed me away. "Get out." Then he pointed the remote at the TV and pressed INSERT.

It was interesting. I always wondered whether I vanished or faded out when I did it. Now I knew. Harold vanished instantly. I looked at the TV. Yup—there he was, right in the middle of his favorite show. Harold was a real Trek fan.

Too bad he'd decided to insert himself in a scene that showed nothing but space. Too bad he didn't have a space suit. It was pretty messy, and I couldn't stand to watch. I walked over to the TV and changed the channel by hand. I guess I'll be doing a lot of that until I can get the folks to buy another remote.

I sure hope it comes with all the same features.

THE SMELL OF DEATH

It was in the air again. I noticed it when I got home from baseball practice. That smell of death. There was no mistake. Dad had sprayed the lawn. Death to the weeds. Death to the bad bugs. Death to the good bugs, too, I guess, but that was part of the cost of victory.

"Spray the lawn again?" I asked Dad when I walked into the open garage where he was putting away a yellow bucket with a black skull and crossbones printed on the side. I figured the stuff was either poison or it was made by pirates.

"You bet," Dad said. "Have to stay on top of unwanted vegetation, or the lawn will get out of control. Can't let the weeds take over. Once they do, it's almost impossible to get rid of them. And the battle against insect pests requires eternal vigilance. Let your guard down, and they'll devour anything green."

"Uh-huh." I was tempted to ask Dad why he didn't just let everything alone. Maybe the insects would eat the weeds. But I had a feeling he wouldn't appreciate the question, so I went inside and plunked down in front of the television. Even with the windows closed, I could still catch a faint whiff of chemicals. But after an hour or so, I didn't notice it anymore. I guess I got used to it.

A week later, I found Dad crawling across the lawn, taking a close look at the flowers that bordered the walkway along the front of the house.

"Lose something?" I asked.

"It's those darned bugs," he said. "Look what they're doing to my *Alstroemeria.*"

I looked over his shoulder at the flowers I assumed must be the Astromania, or whatever it was he called them. They didn't look very flowery. Something had been munching down on them like they were a bag of chips. "Didn't you just spray?" I asked.

Dad nodded.

"Better get your money back," I told him. "The stuff isn't any good."

"It's fine," he said. "The bugs must have developed an immunity to it."

"Huh?" I asked, getting the sinking feeling that I was back in my first period science class with Mr. Calahan. I half expected Dad to pull out a chart and some plastic models.

"It's like this," he said. "A spray will kill most of the bugs. But some of the bugs survive. They just have a natural ability that keeps the spray from hurting them. And some of them pass on that ability to the next generation."

"Like I got Mom's nose?" I asked.

"Yeah." Dad nodded. "Next thing you know, all the bugs

have resistance. So it's time to switch to a different spray. Ideally, the proper technique—"

"Got it," I said, cutting him off before he launched into a long discussion. I understood the basic concept. Some bugs just weren't hurt by a certain spray. Whatever it was about them that caused this, it could be passed along to their little bug kids. And each time Dad sprayed, and each time the bugs had kids, the spray did less and less damage, until it was pretty much completely useless. In a twisted sort of way, Dad was helping the bugs get stronger each time he tried to kill them.

I didn't give it much thought at first, but it was hard to ignore. Every week or two, I'd find Dad spraying something new, and I figured there were enough types of spray around so he'd never run out. Dad would stay happy, and I guess the guy at the hardware store where Dad bought the spray would stay happy. The only ones who wouldn't be happy were the bugs. But the bugs didn't get to vote on the matter.

Then I started thinking about the bugs. And I thought about their immunity. I wondered what else we might be changing. What if it was the stupid bugs who were being killed off? What if the smart bugs had figured a way to survive? Then they'd have smart kid bugs. And those kids— some of them would be smart, and they'd survive. Then they'd have kids. And bugs have kids a lot faster than people have kids, so everything would be speeded up.

No, I decided that was a crazy idea. Bugs were just bugs. Even a smart bug wasn't much brighter than a clump of earwax.

But if they were so dumb, what was going on in the back-yard? I was the first one to notice it. The bugs had crawled from the lawn into a pile. No, it wasn't a pile—it was more like a tube.

I'd never seen bugs like these before. I moved closer to the living tube that was forming in our yard. It was tall enough to reach my chest. I leaned over to get a better look at the insects. They were a bit like beetles, but each one had an extra section—it was sort of like a small rubber ball. The sections pointed toward the inside of the tube.

"Dad," I called, "you've got a ton of bugs out here."

"Where?" Dad came running, armed with his latest spray. He let them have it. It might as well have been water. They didn't even seem to notice.

Then they let loose with their own spray. A greenish cloud drifted out from the tube—puffing out from each bug's extra sections and drifting through the air. I knew right away it was bad stuff.

"Run," Dad said.

We headed for the front yard. But when we got there, we saw another cloud of gas spreading out from the Rathman's yard across the street.

I looked to the left. Several more bug tubes were spread-ing their poison.

I looked to the right. The air was so clouded I couldn't see anything.

There was nowhere to run. There was nothing to do. The cloud drifted over us. The smell—so sweet it made me sick—got everything inside my head spinning around. I dropped to my knees, too weak to walk or even crawl. After a while, the cloud thinned out and I got fresh air into my lungs.

Dad was on the ground next to me. "Are you okay?" he asked.

"Yeah." I got up slowly and looked around. We'd survived. We'd been immune to the spray. This time.

I walked over to the backyard. The bugs were gone. I wondered whether they'd return with a different spray. Maybe, if we left them alone, they'd leave us alone.

"Darn bugs," Dad said as he ran toward the garage. "I'll get something stronger. That'll show them. I'll kill them all this time."

I watched Dad drive off. I understood why he wanted to kill them all. But I knew that wouldn't happen. We'd end up killing the weak ones, while the survivors kept working, breeding another generation for their side of this war. Beneath my feet, the ground seemed to hum with activity. A breeze brought fresh, cool air, dispersing the last traces of the poison. I took a deep breath, enjoying it while I could.

THE SHORTCUT

Lucas felt like he was drowning. The water was pouring down so hard that it was almost a solid force. He could barely see Chuck. "You idiot!" he shouted toward the shape of his friend.

"I didn't think it would rain," Chuck shouted back.

"Idiot," Lucas said again. He couldn't believe he'd listened to Chuck. He couldn't believe how wet he was.

"This way," Chuck said. "We can cut through here." He pointed to the front entrance of Merrydale Hospital.

"What good will that do?" Lucas asked.

"The new section," Chuck said. "We can cut across, and get all the way over to Perry Street. It will save us three blocks. And it'll get us out of the rain."

Lucas followed Chuck through the doors. The sudden shelter was almost as much of a shock as the sudden storm. For a moment, he just stood and dripped, angry with himself for letting Chuck talk him into walking home. It had seemed like a good idea at the time—they could take the long way through town and stop at the arcade. But the downpour had turned the adventure into a disaster.

"Let's get moving," Chuck said. He grabbed Lucas by the arm and headed down a corridor. Their wet sneakers squeaked against the floor.

"We shouldn't be here," Lucas said. To one side of the lobby, he saw a guard. The guard caught his eye and started to walk over. Lucas hurried down the hall. "I think the guard spotted us," he whispered to Chuck.

"That's okay," Chuck said. "There's no rule that says we can't be here. It's a public place."

Lucas followed Chuck, who headed down a stairway next to a row of elevators. "I think this will get us over to the other side," Chuck said.

"Are you sure?" Lucas asked.

"Yeah."

They reached another corridor. Lucas heard footsteps on the stairs. "Someone's following us," he said.

"That's silly," Chuck told him. "Who would—"

"Hey, you kids! Stop!" The voice came from behind them.

Lucas froze for a second. Chuck started running. Lucas made up his mind and ran to catch up with Chuck. They turned a corner at the end of the hallway.

"In here," Chuck said. He dashed through a pair of swinging doors.

Lucas followed. They could hide until the guard was gone, then get out of the hospital. He crouched next to the door, trying not to let his heart beat so loudly that it gave away their hiding place. He couldn't believe all the trouble they were getting into because of one simple shortcut.

In the hallway, he could hear running steps. The steps stopped just outside the door. A face peered through the small window in the door. Lucas scrunched down even lower. He looked over at Chuck, who put his fingers to his lips and went, "Sssshhhhh."

Lucas nodded. The guard glanced down. Then he pushed at the door. It swung inward. "They know better than to leave this open," the guard said. The door closed. There was a jangle of keys. Then there was a worse sound.

Click.

A bolt slid in place as the guard locked the door. He turned away. Lucas heard him chuckle, then say, "Of course, there's no way those kids went in there. No way at all."

He walked off.

No way? Lucas wondered what he meant. For the first time, he looked around the room.

"Oh no . . ." In the middle of the room, Lucas saw four tables. Three were empty. One had something on it. There was a sheet over the table, but it didn't hide the fact that the shape underneath was human.

Across the room, Lucas saw a wall filled with drawers— like file cabinets, but a lot larger and made of stainless steel.

Lucas reached up and pushed against the door. It didn't open. "We're locked in," he said.

Chuck nodded.

"You know what this place is?" Lucas asked.

Chuck nodded again. "Do you?"

"Yeah." Lucas didn't want to use the word "morgue."

"Hey, no big deal," Chuck said. "We all end up here sooner or later."

Behind him, Lucas heard a slithery sound. He spun, flattening against the wall. On the table in front of him, an arm had slipped down. A hand poked out from beneath the sheet.

"It moved!" Lucas shouted.

"Calm down," Chuck said. "It's dead. It can't do anything to us."

Lucas stared at the hand, waiting for it to move again. But it didn't. "Stupid shortcut," he said, glaring at Chuck.

Chuck shrugged. "I didn't know . . ."

Lucas looked toward the door again. There were more footsteps in the hallway. He looked right out the window this time—less afraid of being caught than of being locked in the morgue. *This can't get any worse*, he thought. At the end of the hall, he saw someone who looked like a custodian. The guy was carrying a mop, wearing headphones, and bobbing his head as he walked. Lucas realized the guy was listening to music. When he turned the corner, he reached out and flipped a wall switch.

The lights went out.

The hall was pitch-black. The morgue was pitch-black. There were no windows. Lucas lost it. "HELP!" he screamed, slamming against the door. "WE'RE LOCKED IN!"

He kept screaming and banging. It seemed like he'd shouted forever. Finally, his voice nearly gone, his throat hoarse, Lucas realized something was missing. Nobody else was screaming.

"Chuck?"

No answer . . .

"Come on, Chuck, say something." Lucas listened for Chuck. He tried to hold his breath, but he was still winded from his burst of panic and couldn't keep from panting. He put his back against the wall and sat. "Chuck, this isn't funny."

Okay, he told himself. *I'll wait.* He wasn't going to play Chuck's stupid game. He was just going to sit and wait. Sooner or later, Chuck would talk to him again. *Unless something happened to Chuck while I was screaming,* Lucas thought. But that was ridiculous. He tried to keep that thought out of his mind while he waited.

After a while, a sound broke the dead silence. It was the sound of a drawer sliding open—a large drawer.

"Stop that, Chuck!"

Another drawer opened. And another.

"If I catch you, I'm going to beat the snot out of you," Lucas said. He'd had enough. He stood and held his arms out. He was going to find Chuck. Lucas took a step away from the wall and tried to remember exactly how the room looked. There were tables in the middle. Lucas shuddered. He didn't want to think about going near the one with the body. Especially not in the dark.

Lucas decided to work his way around the walls first. He put his hand out, feeling the cool tiles. Still listening for any hint of Chuck's location, Lucas started to make his way around the room. He held one hand against the wall and the other in front of him.

Lucas reached the corner. He heard another drawer slide open.

He worked his way along the side wall, then crept to the back wall. More drawers slid open. He dropped to his hands and knees and started to crawl along the floor so he wouldn't run into an open drawer. Chuck had to be close by.

Lucas crept silently toward the spot where he'd heard the last drawer open. His hand brushed against something. It was a shoe. "Gotcha!" Lucas said, grabbing the leg.

Shoe?

Chuck wore sneakers.

Lucas froze. He tried to detect any sense of life in the leg he clutched. The skin beneath the pants felt dead and cold. Lucas let go and leaped to his feet. He didn't quite make it. His head crashed into the bottom of an open drawer. As he dropped to the floor, he felt hands grab him. The world was fading. The darkness of the room was being swallowed by a deeper darkness.

"You weren't supposed to arrive here for many years," one voice whispered.

"You're ahead of schedule," another said.

Someone nearby laughed. "Looks like you took a shortcut."

A WORD OR TWO ABOUT THESE STORIES

"Where do you get your ideas?" This is probably the most common question every writer gets asked. For me, there's not one simple answer. Every story takes a different path. Some ideas appear in a flash. Others grow slowly. Here's a behind-the-scenes look at the various ways I got the ideas for the stories in this collection.

"The Last Halloween"

As the father of a growing (and almost grown) daughter, I've always wondered when she would outgrow Halloween. Happily, it seems like that time will never come. But the thought of a girl on the verge of being too old to trick-or-treat gave rise to this story. It's one of my favorites to read aloud. I especially like it because Jennifer refuses to be a victim.

"Bed Tings"

My grandmother talked with an accent. One day, I was thinking about the phrase "Bad Things Come in Threes," and the word "three" spawned a memory of the way she said "tree" instead. She was a cool grandmother. She watched wrestling, played poker, and dressed up and wore white gloves when she went to the supermarket. As far as I know, she didn't climb trees.

"The Dead Won't Hurt You"

I started with the opening scene, and no idea what would happen. I just wanted to put a creeped-out kid in the middle of a cemetery at midnight. I figured something interesting would pop up. When I was younger, I felt spooked by cemeteries, but they don't bother me now. At least, not as much.

"Copies"

Our local schools get very involved in Take Our Kids to Work Day. That was on my mind when I started writing this story. Sometimes, readers ask me what happened in a story after the ending. In this case, I don't think anybody is going to want to think about that. Ick.

"Shaping the Fog"

This was one of those stories that just showed up. I have no idea what inspired it, but I'm so glad it appeared. I'd like to think I was staring out my window at fog that day. But maybe I was just in a fog of my own. I don't think I've written anything else quite like it. Whatever magic is involved in the creation of stories like this, it is as elusive as a handful of mist.

"Willard's Oppositional Notebook"

There's a long tradition of stories where a powerful object brings disaster to its owner. I'd been thinking of various objects that might grant wishes. First, I thought of a pencil. That led me to notebooks. But I didn't want the notebook to just grant wishes, so I kept thinking until I came up with a satisfying twist.

"A Tiny Little Piece"
There are always people who think the rules don't apply to them, and people who don't think it will matter if they steal just a tiny piece of something like a coral reef or historical object. That's what was on my mind when I started writing this one. As you can tell from the story, I think it matters. But then again, when it comes to following the rules, I'm a bit of a weenie.

"The La Brea Toy Pits"
This idea came purely as a pun based on the La Brea Tar Pits. Once the idea of toy pits grabbed me, it was easy to write the story. Puns are always running through my mind. There's no way I can stop them, so I might as well make use of them. I just have to remember to keep from saying too many of them out loud, or I'll be asked to leave the room.

"Mr. Lambini's Haunted House"
There's one person in every neighborhood who goes all out on Halloween and creates a haunted house. I've watched kids who are too scared to enter, and others who make a big show of how brave they are. This gave rise to wondering what would happen if there were more to the house than anyone knew.

"Numbskull"

We each have an inner censor that keeps us from saying the wrong stuff. Mine doesn't always work. I started to wonder what would happen to a kid if a shot of novocaine numbed that censor. Despite this story, I like my dentist.

"A Little Night Fishing"

The first time I went night fishing, I knew the experience would make a great setting for a story. I tried to capture the feeling of moving through dark woods and standing on the edge of moonlit water. All fishing is tinged with a sense of the mystic, but this feeling becomes especially intense at night. I caught a bat that evening, but that's another story.

"Precious Memories"

I've always been amused by people who spend so much time taping an event that they never actually see it for real. And, of course, technology is a rich area for strange twists. We use this stuff, and we know it works, but sometimes it might as well be magic. And magic doesn't always work the way we expect.

"Baby Talk"

I started out thinking what it would be like for a kid if her baby brother became famous. That, of course, led me to wonder, famous for what? This is a good example of how one idea can lead to another.

"Unseen"

I used to walk with my eyes closed to see if I could tell when I was about to reach something. I never went as far as our unfortunate main character, and I'd never be foolish enough to try to cross the street. I haven't done it in a while. But the way my eyesight is, I might as well be walking around with my eyes closed anyhow.

"Flyers"

I started out with the idea that someone finds a flyer that says 10 PERCENT OFF, and then the world seems 10 percent smaller. It was pretty easy to come up with all sorts of other flyers after that. Feel free to give it a try yourself, and see what you come up with. Maybe you can find a different way to end the story.

"Every Autumn"

I was thinking about piles of leaves by the curb, and the way kids walk through them. This is another example of something ordinary (at least if you live where there are deciduous trees) becoming something strange.

"Goose Eggs"

I was wondering what would happen if a couple kids really did get their hands on golden eggs. And I've always felt that geese are vicious. Putting that together, it wasn't hard to figure out what was really behind—or inside of—those eggs.

"Fresh from the Garden"

Another idea harvested from my "what if" collection. I guess I was thinking about the various fish buried in my backyard, not all that far from the tomatoes. Yum.

"The Covered Bridge"

There are half a zillion covered bridges in Pennsylvania. They're pretty cool, but they can also be a bit creepy. Fear is a natural element for spooky stories.

"Buzz Off"

We've all been there—a bee lands on you and you freeze, wondering whether to hit it or wait for it to fly away. I just decided to take things to an absurd place. That's one of the joys of short stories—you can get as weird as you want.

"Just Desserts"

I love fishing, but I'd much rather wade a local river than travel for hours to reach the ocean, and then travel more hours on a boat to get to some hot spot where the bluefish might be biting. The two deep-sea trips I've taken inspired me to put a kid on a boat and see what happened. As for the pie, I'll pick cherry, and I'll eat it first.

"The Whole Nine Yards"

After seeing lots of concrete with initials and other writing, I started thinking about what else you might see. Footprints came to mind. This is a good example of a technique I use a lot. I'll set up a problem or puzzle, and then write a story to explain it. This way, both I and the reader are in for a surprise.

"The Green Man"

When I was in elementary school, everyone was talking about the Green Man. We were truly spooked about him, and I remember looking over my shoulder when I walked anywhere. They said he had a collie with him. He was spotted on the roof of the school once. It was a strange sort of dread. I knew he couldn't be real, but he still haunted me. I tried to capture that feeling in this story.

"Dizzy Spells"

Yet another idea right out of my "what if" file. As is often the case, I started out with a concept—dizziness leads to granted wishes—and just let the idea grow and take shape as I wrote.

"The Tank"

My house has a septic tank. I try not to think about it too much, but as you can see, I can't always control the directions my mind takes. And I can't help noticing the ripples in the water.

"Anything You Want"

Another journey without a map. I wanted to write about a kid finding a genie. I guess that combined in my mind with the whole idea of things being misheard.

"Lines"

I was visiting an elementary school and noticed how kids are always moving from place to place in a line. From there, it was easy to wonder "what if someone stepped out of line?" The most commonplace things can spark a story if you look at them with fresh eyes.

"Wandering Stu"

If you go into just about any school library, you'll probably see at least a couple hanging plants. More often than not, the plant is a variety of Wandering Jew. I guess I was staring at one of those when the phrase "Wandering Stu" floated through my mind. I knew I had to come up with a tale to fit the title. It wasn't hard to dream up a way to make Stu wander. Mean kids are often the most fun to write about.

"Tarnation"

Little kids have their own amazing mythology about things like monsters. I liked the idea of a little kid getting involved in something that actually worked. Of course, I liked it even better when I realized how it could backfire.

"Ten Pounds of Chocolate"

Every Halloween, I hear kids passing the word about which houses give out the biggest candy bars. The news almost takes on the feel of a legend. I'd been playing around with a different idea, about Halloween candy that turns into something bad, but when I started thinking about big bars of chocolate, it led me in a new direction.

"The Boy Who Wouldn't Talk"

I get a lot of ideas by thinking about things that don't quite fit into the normal world. There always seems to be one kid in each class who doesn't talk. The fun part is figuring out why.

"Invasion of the Road Weenies"

Like the character in the story, I noticed that adult joggers never smile. As I started wondering about this, I realized that something must be making them jog. This was the best explanation I could come up with.

"We Interrupt This Program"

I think I was playing with the remote when I got this idea. There were actually a couple buttons hidden under a sliding panel. There was nothing as exciting as "insert." It was just stuff like a sleep timer (which I never figured out how to use, or even had any desire to use). Mundane or not, those buttons gave me the idea.

"The Smell of Death"

I've always been concerned about the excessive use of pesticides, and amused by the people who are so in love with their lawns that they will wash themselves in chemicals for the sake of grass that looks nicer than the neighbors'. (See *In the Land of the Lawn Weenies* for another example of this.)

"The Shortcut"

I remember getting caught in a major rainstorm when I was a kid. When I started writing this story, all I had in mind was a couple of very wet kids. Once they walked into the hospital, it was easy to know where to send them. I try to end every collection with a really scary story. I hope this one did the trick.

Well, that wraps up this collection. Now that I've covered lawn weenies and road weenies, I need to think about who might be next. Maybe those all-too-serious guys in their funny shorts and high-tech helmets who don't know that bicycles are supposed to be fun. Hmmm . . . bike weenies . . . Now there's an idea I can sink my mind into.